HAZE

orca sports

HAZE

ERIN THOMAS

ORCA BOOK PUBLISHERS

Library and Archives Canada Cataloguing in Publication

Thomas, E. L. (Erin L.)
Haze / Erin Thomas.
(Orca sports)

Issued also in electronic formats.
ISBN 978-1-4598-0070-0

I. Title. II. Series: Orca sports
PS8639.H572H39 2012   jC813'.6   C2011-907783-3

First published in the United States, 2012
Library of Congress Control Number: 2011943721

Summary: When trouble arises on Bram's swim team, he struggles
to find out who hurt his friend and to protect his coach from blame.

*Orca Book Publishers is dedicated to preserving the environment and has
printed this book on paper certified by the Forest Stewardship Council®.*

Orca Book Publishers gratefully acknowledges the support for its publishing
programs provided by the following agencies: the Government of Canada
through the Canada Book Fund and the Canada Council for the Arts, and the
Province of British Columbia through the BC Arts Council and
the Book Publishing Tax Credit.

Cover photography by Getty Images
Author photo by Neil Kinnear and Lesley Chung

ORCA BOOK PUBLISHERS
PO Box 5626, Stn. B
Victoria, BC Canada
V8R 6S4

ORCA BOOK PUBLISHERS
PO Box 468
Custer, WA USA
98240-0468

www.orcabook.com
Printed and bound in Canada.

15 14 13 12 • 4 3 2 1

For Mike, the crusader of the family,
with love and apologies for years of
bad nicknames.

chapter one

I curled the toes of my left foot around the cool concrete edge of the starting block. My right foot was behind me, ready to push.

I was trying out for the Strathmore Academy swim team along with a bunch of other kids. Most of them were ninth graders, a year younger than me. The Sharks called us "pond scum."

I breathed deep, like I always did before a race, filling my nose with the smell of chlorine. The Sharks were about to see that this pond scum could swim.

I bent forward. My fingers skimmed the starting block. My lane was in front of me, blue water rippling. This was my world. I was focused. Ready.

"Go!"

The Sharks hadn't even finished shouting the word before I sliced the air in a dive. I broke water, not going too deep, dolphin-kicking up to the surface to keep my speed. My arms pulled me through the water, fighting the drag of the adult-sized diaper I wore over my swimsuit.

The diapers were for us pond scum. Just like the Vaseline-in-the-swim-cap joke. Or the time they stole our clothes out of the locker room and we had to walk across the grounds and back to the dorms in our Speedos.

Compared to the Speedo walk, wearing diapers for this race wasn't that bad. Mine was soaking up water fast, slowing me down. It didn't matter. I didn't have to beat my personal best. I only had to beat the other pond scum.

To make the team, I had to impress Coach. But to be *part* of the team, I had to impress the Sharks.

I was in the outside left lane, so I couldn't tell what the other swimmers were doing, except for Droid, my roommate. He had the lane beside mine. Droid was a strong swimmer, but faster on his back than on his front. Back crawl was his stroke. The front crawl was mine. I passed him.

I shot my arms out again and again. My shoulders burned because my body wasn't slicing through the water like it usually did.

Droid fell behind. The wall was in front of me. I forced my body down and around and dolphin-kicked up again, never breaking my stride. This was a short race, only four lengths.

The soggy diaper slid down over my hips, strangling my kick. My arms were churning water, not slicing through it. I sucked in a quick gulp of air and powered on to the end of the pool. Two more lengths.

By the time I finished, the diaper had slipped down almost to my knees.

I tagged the wall and surfaced in one motion, looking to the right to see the others finish. Droid was a few strokes back. One other guy, with a bright red swim cap, was already holding the wall. I didn't know his name. Most of these guys, even the ninth-grade freshmen, knew each other. They were all connected through Connecticut rich-boy clubs or whatever. Not me. I was the scholarship kid.

Red Cap pumped a fist in the air, letting me know he had won. Not surprising. His shoulders were about six feet wide. When it came down to a power race, like this one with the drag of the diapers, he had all of us beat.

Still, second wasn't bad.

"Out of the pool, pond scum," one of the Sharks called. It was Steven, the one who always looked as if he had stepped out of a J.Crew ad. All the other swimmers had finished. We were never more than a few seconds apart from each other.

Coach Gordon leaned against the swim team office's large window. A row of trophies was lined up on a ledge behind him. His Olympic silver wasn't there though. That he kept at home.

He gave me a nod, letting me know he had been watching and that he liked what he had seen. I grinned, but ducked under the water to hide it. He wasn't even supposed to be here. It was tradition—he usually disappeared for the last fifteen minutes of each tryout session and let the Sharks run things. That was where the diapers came in.

If he had stuck around to watch the hazing, he had a reason. We hauled ourselves onto the tiles and waited to hear what Coach had to say.

chapter two

As I stood beside Droid, in line with the other pond scum, one of the Sharks, Jeremy Blackburn, gave me a thumbs-up. That was as close as he could come to saying "Good race, Bram." My chest puffed up.

Jeremy was a senior-year swimmer from my hometown, Storrs. He was here on a scholarship too. I had grown up chasing his swimming records. Some I beat, some I never managed to. I'd never admit it to him, but when I was eight and he was ten,

I told my mom I wanted to be Jeremy when I grew up.

I even dated his sister, Abby, back in grade eight. That kind of put a downer on the whole hero-worship thing. Before she decided we were better off as friends, Abby told me all of Jeremy's disgusting habits, like the fact that he picks his toes when he watches television.

What mattered more than the thumbs-up from Jeremy, though, was the nod from Coach Gordon. He was the reason I was here.

"Nice uniforms," Coach Gordon joked, addressing the line of us standing on the pool deck with soppy diapers hanging around our hips. "Boys, I thought I told you not to be too hard on them." This last bit was directed at the Sharks. Mostly at Steven.

Steven's face might as well have been molded from plastic. His best friend, Nate, poked him in the ribs. Nate wore a towel around his shoulders like a cape.

"You've all worked hard to be here," Coach said. "Tomorrow's practice will be our last tryout. It'll be at the Yale pool, not here. Those of you who have been around the team will know Yale has an Olympic-length pool, so we practice there once a week. I want to see what you boys can do with a decent stretch of water in front of you. Sunday, you can check my office door for the team list. Before we go, I want you to know that it has been a privilege working with each and every one of you."

He looked at each of us in turn. His eyes stayed on me for an extra second. What did that mean? Did it mean I made the team? Did it mean I was out? I had come to Strathmore on one of their swimming scholarships, but Coach made it clear from the start I had to earn my way to the team like everyone else.

But if I didn't make the team this year, no scholarship next year. My parents couldn't afford Strathmore tuition. And then there would be no chance to attract the attention of the college scouts, who always watched the Strathmore team.

Swimming was my ticket to a good college. It was all I had.

Coach was still speaking. "They say swimming is an individual sport. But that's not the way we do it here at Strathmore, is it, boys?"

We knew our cue. "Go Sharks!"

Coach grinned. "I see good things ahead, team. Very good things."

He headed out of the pool area, tugging his belt up over the slightest hint of a pot belly. I wondered what he meant. Good things? Did we have a shot at statewide this year? Nationals, even?

"Is that clear, pond scum?"

I jumped at Steven's shout. I had missed something. Coach was gone, and Steven was glaring at us. He wasn't officially in charge of the Sharks, but they let him take the lead. Maybe it had to do with his being head boy. At my old school, a title like that would have been social suicide. Here, it seemed to mean something.

"Psst. Dude." Droid stepped on my foot.

I nodded and said, "Yes, Shark Steven," with the others. Trying not to be obvious,

I looked to see what the other pond scum were doing. One by one, they walked toward the sauna. Waddled might be a better word. Apparently it wasn't time to remove the diaper yet. Too bad, because it chafed.

This was a favorite game of the Sharks. Stick us in the sauna, lock it from outside until we half melted, and then make us run and jump into the water. The pool wasn't warm at the best of times, but after ten minutes in the sauna, it felt like a polar bear dip.

I took a seat on one of the lowest benches, figuring it wouldn't get quite as hot. With twelve of us packed in together, it was crowded.

"Loving the new swimsuits," Droid said, taking a spot on the bench beside me. Water dripped from his hair. He had dyed it blue, but he never wore a swim cap. The chlorine four times a week was bleaching it a weird green color. Between his washed-out green hair and his thick dark eyebrows, Droid was hard to miss.

I shifted and the diaper squelched. "They're chick magnets," I said. I hoped the Sharks wouldn't steal our clothes this time. The rest of the school would be up by now. My boys didn't like the cold, and a Speedo didn't do much to hide that fact.

"Hey—they're leaving!" It was Red Cap. He was on the top bench, taking up twice as much room as anyone else.

I peered through the narrow glass window over the door handle. Sure enough, Jeremy and Steven were disappearing through the locker-room door. No one else was in sight. The last time they packed us into the sauna, somebody had stayed behind to let us out. "They'll be back," I said. Sweat rolled down my face.

"They'd better be," Red Cap said. "It's hot in here."

"It is a sauna," Droid pointed out.

"Oh, really, boy genius?" Red Cap said. "I hadn't noticed." He flopped back against the wall, then sat up fast. "This sucks."

"Jeremy won't leave us in here," I said. And sure enough, a few minutes later,

11

the locker-room door opened again. Jeremy was wearing his pissed-off look and walking fast. He almost slipped on the tile.

"Nice move, Shark," Red Cap said.

"Shut up. He's letting us out," I said.

Jeremy opened the door. "Two lengths," he said, with a halfhearted wave toward the pool. Some of the guys booed. They would never have done that with Steven.

I was the last out. Jeremy put a hand on my arm to stop me. He glanced around to make sure no one was listening. "Bram—be careful, okay? Don't do anything stupid, no matter who asks you to. And don't go to the initiation party."

Before I could ask what he meant, Red Cap spotted us. "Hey, pond scum! I don't care what your boyfriend says, you have to get in the pool with the rest of us." He cannonballed into the water, still wearing his diaper.

I followed, but chucked the diaper like most of the others had done. The cold water shocked my skin into goose bumps.

I concentrated on swimming hard and beating Red Cap. By the time I finished my lengths, Jeremy was gone.

chapter three

I tracked Jeremy down in the weight room that evening. It was late enough that we had the room to ourselves. Not a lot of people like to spend Friday night in a windowless, concrete-walled basement room in glamorous Strathmore Academy.

"What are you doing here?" Jeremy said.

"I'm fifteen, nothing better to do," I said, adjusting the leg press to two hundred pounds, a little more than I usually pressed. Jeremy might not have been the one choosing the team, but he was still a Shark. "What's your excuse?"

Jeremy had a car, even if it was a clunker compared to the sixteenth-birthday BMWs that littered Strathmore's parking lot. He had options.

He finished his set before answering. He was doing pull-downs, working on his arms. "Not in the mood to go out, I guess," he said.

I let him finish another set of ten pull-downs before interrupting. "So...what's with the warning?" It was all I could do to keep the weights from crashing down. Maybe two hundred was too much.

"We both know you're going to make the team," he said as his pulley slid up and down. "Just skip the party, all right? Make an excuse."

I pushed out again. My leg muscles shook as the weights rose into the air. "You can't" –breathe–"just"–breathe–"say that." I let the weight down, slowly. "You have to explain."

The party was going to be at Steven's friend Nate's house. Rumor had it Nate's parents were away and the place was well stocked. Some girls from our sister school, Wallingford, were going to be there too. Wallingford was an all-girls boarding school, like Strathmore was for boys, except the girls wore kilts.

And kneesocks.

Jeremy walked over to look at what I was lifting. "You should focus on what you're doing," he said. "This is too much weight for you."

"I can handle it." I groaned, pushing out again.

"Uh-huh," he said. But this time, when I lowered the weight, he tugged out the key that kept the weights together.

I pushed again, and my legs flew out. The default weight was only twenty pounds. "Hey! I'm not a girl."

He raised an eyebrow. "I dare you to say that to Abby."

"Yeah, right," I said. Abby would deck me, or worse. The girl carried a knife. A thumb-sized Swiss Army knife, but still.

I held out my hand. "Give me back the pin."

"Nope." He stuck it back in the weight rack, several weights lighter than where I'd had it. "Try that. Should be around your body weight. Work with that."

I worked my legs, slow and steady, concentrating on my form. "Better?"

"Always listen to your elders," he said.

I finished my set at the lower weight. "Except when the elders tell you to miss a party and won't tell you why."

He sighed and went over to the mats to stretch. "You ever hear of Marcus Tam?"

I shook my head.

"You would have, if he'd lived. He would have an Olympic medal in freestyle by now."

Olympic is a big word, and Jeremy wouldn't just throw it around. This kid must have been good. "So what happened to him?" I started another set. Jeremy had been right about the weights. It was better like this.

"Initiation party," Jeremy said. "My first year. Things got out of hand. And instead of taking him to the hospital like they probably should have, the older guys dropped him off back here in his room to sleep it off." He turned his back to me and started looking through the free weights. I don't know if he was really seeing them though. He picked up the same five-pound weight three times. "He choked on his own vomit and died."

"Oh," I said. I'd heard of stuff like that happening, but never to anyone real, if that makes sense. I mean, of course they were real people, but they weren't connected to anyone I knew. "Were you friends?"

Jeremy tensed. "Roommates," he said finally. "So if I'd gone home with..."

"You can't know that," I said. "You can't know what would have happened."

He shrugged and turned to face me again. "Anyhow, it was all hushed up. Not that he died, obviously, but that it was an initiation party. The hazing and all that stuff—nobody talked about it. The stuff in the papers made it sound like he was some kind of binge drinker or something.

A dumb kid let loose on his own for the first time, drinking underage. Nothing about the team, except that he happened to be a swimmer. The school took some heat and did room inspections more often for a while. And the swim team was really careful the next year. No hazing, no initiation. But last year, it started up again. And this year...let's just say I know the pattern."

"I'm not stupid," I said. "And besides, you'll be there, right? We can make sure nothing bad happens."

He shook his head. "You don't understand. I'm not worried about some random accident. They know we're friends, and they said if I—"

He slammed his mouth shut as if he wanted to bite back the words.

I lowered the weight slowly. The room seemed to shrink. "If you what?"

He shook his head. "I'll make sure nothing happens. It's time to come clean about what happened to Marcus. I've talked to some of the other guys—"

The door swung open as he was speaking. It was Steven. Nate was right behind him. Jeremy's face went white.

"Don't let us interrupt," Steven said.

Jeremy straightened. "We were just talking about Bram's kick. It needs work."

My eyebrows reached for my hairline.

Nate shrugged. "Kid hasn't made the team yet. Worry about it when he does."

It was like I wasn't even in the room. "Uh, hello? Still here," I said.

"Watch your tone, pond scum," Steven said. "Drop and give me fifty." He turned to Jeremy. "We need to talk. Privately."

We weren't at the pool. So technically, he couldn't boss me around. But I didn't want to get into it with him. I held his eyes until he glanced away, then I got down on the floor.

I took my time with the push-ups. All the way up and all the way down, so slowly my arms shook. If Steven wanted to talk to Jeremy privately, I wasn't going to make it easy for him.

When I finished, Nate grinned. "Nicely done, pond scum. You made your point," he said. "Now give us a sec, okay? Shark business."

I stood up and looked at Jeremy. "You want me to leave?"

"It's fine," he said. "See you in the morning for our run?"

What run? "Uh, sure," I said, as he jerked his head toward Nate and Steven.

"Six o'clock. Out front, by the flagpole. Don't be late," he said.

I waited outside the weight room. If I heard anything like a struggle, I was going back in.

Jeremy was the first one out. He frowned when he saw me standing there. "What are you doing?"

"Nothing," I said, stung. Didn't he realize I had waited for him?

Jeremy opened his mouth to say something, but the door opened again, letting Nate and Steven out. Nate winked at me. "Good kid."

I'd had enough of all three of them. "You done? Can I use the room? Some of us have training to do."

A look flickered across Jeremy's face. It vanished too quickly for me to read it. "Remember what I told you," he said. "Less weight. It might make a difference."

I headed inside and made a few attempts to get started, but my head wasn't in it.

Time to come clean. Maybe. But I was here to swim. I didn't want to be part of anybody's crusade. Not even for Jeremy.

chapter four

I woke up to loud beeping. My head felt thick, like I was still half stuck in a dream.

I sat up and rubbed my eyes. Time to meet Jeremy. Time to find out what he was going to tell me before Steven had interrupted. And time to let Jeremy know that, whatever he was planning to do, I couldn't be a part of it.

Droid sighed and rolled over as I smacked the alarm. His side of the room was all *Star Wars* posters and glowing computer equipment. That, and a giant Mexican flag over his headboard.

I dressed in the dark while planning what to say to Jeremy. I needed a spot on this team. The Sharks were jerks, but I couldn't afford to piss them off, or Coach. What happened to Marcus was tragic, but it was in the past. The police had done their bit. If anyone was at fault, it would have been dealt with by now. Jeremy needed to move on.

Maybe I wouldn't say that last bit to his face.

I jammed a ballcap over my bed-head and jogged downstairs.

At Strathmore, we were allowed to go for early morning runs or walks as long as we signed out and got back in time for breakfast. The sign-out book sat on a dark wooden table outside the headmaster's office. I flipped to a new page, wrote today's date at the top and signed my name. Jeremy hadn't signed out yet.

Outside, I walked back and forth between the front steps and the nearest lamppost to keep warm. It wasn't breath-frosting chilly, not yet, but my arms were all goose bumps. I stretched my calves, leaning each foot in turn against the concrete steps. A jack-o'-lantern sat on the top step, its hollow eyes following me.

I waited five minutes, then ten.

I texted Jeremy and even tried phoning. No answer.

I left the school grounds at a light jog and didn't really start pushing myself until I had passed a few cookie-cutter mansions. My usual five-mile loop took me up around Yale and back to Strathmore in time for breakfast. I passed some woods, then the golf course, and then headed toward downtown New Haven. It started to rain—a light, misty drizzle that felt good on the back of my neck.

On my way back to school, I saw flashing lights up ahead, near the Catholic cemetery. A police cruiser was parked across the road, blocking the way. I detoured past some more monster houses and made it back to school only a little later than usual.

The minute I walked through the dining hall doors for breakfast, I smelled bacon. It took me a minute to notice the quiet. A charged quiet, not a sleepy one.

Some of the Sharks, but not Jeremy, sat huddled around a table in the corner. Nate crumpled a paper napkin while I watched. Steven said something to him, and Nate shook his head.

I finally spotted Droid. He was sitting with Red Cap and some of the other pond scum, not with his usual crowd of computer geeks. I slid into the seat across from him. "What's going on?"

Red Cap stopped mopping up yolk with his toast long enough to look at me. "You don't know yet?"

I got an eyeful of the half-chewed egg in his mouth. "Know what?"

Droid spoke. "It's your friend Jeremy. He was hit by a car this morning. He's in the hospital. Bram, I'm sorry."

No one at the table met my eyes. I gripped the edges of my chair. I needed Droid to keep talking. I needed not to have to ask.

Red Cap swallowed whatever was in his mouth. "They don't know if he's going to make it. Do you think they'll open up another spot on the team?"

chapter five

I still wasn't used to Saturday-morning school, but that was the way they did it at Strathmore. Wednesday afternoons off for athletic training, Saturday morning classes instead. Geography and English passed in a blur, except for the part where the guidance counselor came in to talk about Jeremy's accident and some of the things we might be feeling.

How would she know?

I signed out before lunch and hopped on my bike. Jeremy was at the hospital in downtown New Haven. His family had probably arrived by now. Storrs was just over an hour away. There was nothing I could do that they couldn't. But I had to go.

By the time I reached the hospital, my jacket and jeans were soaked through with rain. I locked my bike and carried my helmet inside. I wanted to shake like a dog and get the water off as I passed between the two sets of glass doors that led to the lobby. I settled for wringing out my jacket.

At the information desk, a gray-haired lady with a volunteer pin on her sweater frowned at me. "Can I help you?" Her eyes flicked to the puddles forming by my feet.

"I'm looking for Jeremy Blackburn," I said.

She pinched her lips and typed something into a computer, never once looking at the keys. "Are you family?" she finally asked.

"Uh, no. Close friend."

"It's family only up in intensive care," she said, and motioned to the next person in line.

I should have lied, but at least now I knew he was in intensive care. The floor plan posted on a wall near the elevators told me I needed to get to the seventh floor.

The elevator ride took forever. When the doors finally slid open on seven, Coach Gordon was there, waiting to get on. He stood with his hands in his pockets, staring into space.

"Coach!"

He blinked like someone waking up. "Bram." He stepped back. "I'll catch the next one."

I tripped over the gap on my way out. "Have you seen Jeremy? How is he?"

"They won't let me in. His parents are inside now." He shook his head. "Terrible thing. But—what are you doing here? Shouldn't you be at the school?"

"It's lunch," I said. But he was right. For something like this, signing out wasn't enough. I should have gotten permission from the headmaster.

Coach studied me for a moment. "It's all right. I'll cover for you," he said. He led me down the hall to where there were some armchairs and a vending machine. "You're a good kid, coming here like this."

I didn't want to hear what a good kid I was. I wanted to hear about Jeremy. "Did they tell you anything?"

Coach sighed and stared at the floor between his feet. "He hit his head pretty bad. There are some other injuries too. He won't be swimming again this year."

"What does that mean, pretty bad?" I asked. Coach had taught a unit on first aid in gym class. Head injuries could kill.

He shook his head. "I'm repeating what the nurse said. And I tell you, I was lucky to get that much out of her." He made a fist and punched it into his open hand. "If I ever get my hands on the bastard who did this..."

"What are you doing here?" It was a girl's voice. One I knew. One I hadn't heard in a long time.

I looked up to see Abby, Jeremy's younger sister. My ex.

chapter six

Abby looked good. That was the first thing that crossed my mind. At least I had the sense not to say it.

She wore a green plaid kilt and a sweater with the Wallingford Collegiate crest. She had cut her hair too, into something chin-length with lots of edges. It suited her. She still had lots of earrings. Three silver hoops in each ear, and a little cuff-thing at the top of her left one.

"Sorry about your brother," I managed.

She nodded and walked over to the vending machine. She seemed to be having trouble getting the coins into the slot. Her hands shook. "Damn it!" Her quarters clattered across the tile floor. One rolled all the way to my shoe.

"Here." I gathered up the coins and fed them into the machine, one by one. Her head hardly came up to my shoulder when she was standing beside me. Her perfume smelled like oranges. "What did you want?"

"Coke." She ducked her head as I handed it to her. "Thanks."

Coach looked from Abby to me and back again. "You two know each other?"

"This is Jeremy's sister, Abby," I said. "Abby, this is—"

"I know." Her voice was cold. I thought that was a bit weird, considering Coach had come here to see how her brother was doing. He obviously cared. It made me feel good about being on his team. She opened the Coke and drank half the can without looking at us.

"I'll...just be going, then," Coach said. He put a hand on my shoulder. "You take it easy, all right? I'll see you back at the pool. And...if anyone hassles you, tell them I gave you permission to visit Jeremy."

I nodded, and then he was gone.

Abby glared after him. "He's got nerve, coming here."

"What are you talking about?" Her brother was hurt, but she didn't need to take it out on Coach.

She dropped into one of the armchairs. I heard the crackling sound of her soda can being squeezed. I lifted it out of her hands.

"I'm here with the Society for the Protection of Coke Cans," I said. "Ma'am, were you aware that this is considered abusive behavior?"

"This is insane." She made a noise somewhere between a laugh and a sob, and buried her head in her arms.

I sat on the arm of the chair beside hers and rubbed her back. "It'll be okay."

When she looked up, her eyes were wet. "You're not supposed to say that. Don't you know? You can't promise."

No, I couldn't. But that wasn't what she needed to hear. "I know your brother," I said. "It's a safe bet."

She sniffed and smiled. "Yeah." She took a deep breath, then dug a wadded-up tissue out of her pocket and dabbed at her face. "Sorry for—"

I shook my head. "Don't say that. You don't have to be sorry for anything right now. It's in the rules."

"There are rules for this?" She was sitting straighter now, looking more like the Abby I remembered.

I nodded seriously. "There's a whole manual. Didn't you read it?"

"Much like in English class, I am woefully unprepared." She rolled her neck from side to side. "What did Coach tell you?"

"Not much. Jeremy hit his head."

"His femurs are both broken," Abby said. "He's going to be mad when he—if he—"

"When," I said.

She nodded, twisting one of her hoop earrings. "There's bleeding in his brain, deep inside. They had to put in a drain. They're going to keep him sedated for a few days. And then, when he wakes up...well, we just have to wait." She took a deep breath. "I should get back to Mom and Dad."

I didn't know what to say. I didn't want her to leave. "Jeremy never said you went to Wallingford." We had talked about home. Even about Abby, once or twice, but he had never mentioned that she was nearby.

She looked down. "I should go."

"Can I see your phone?" I asked. She hesitated, then handed it to me. I programmed in my number. "Call me if there's anything I can do, okay?"

She nodded. She already seemed distracted and looked toward the ICU door.

"Abby?" I said. I waited until she looked at me. "Call me no matter what. Promise."

She pocketed the phone. We stood there, looking at one another. It was time for her to leave, but she didn't. I thought maybe I understood. She wanted to go back into the ICU, but at the same time she didn't.

"Do you need anything?" I asked. "Do you want me to stay? I've got swim practice, but...well, if you needed anything..."

She shook her head.

"I'm sorry about the accident," I said.

She stiffened, and her eyes narrowed. "It wasn't an accident."

"What do you mean?"

"I heard the doctor. Jeremy's injuries are high up. You know what that means? The car didn't brake. The bastard didn't even slow down."

chapter seven

On Saturday afternoons, we practiced at the Yale pool. It was an Olympic-length pool, unlike the one at Strathmore. Droid and I usually biked there together. Today, though, I raced from the hospital to make it on time.

No chance for lunch. My hands shook. I was hungry and tired going into our last tryout session. But Coach would understand if I wasn't up to speed. Wouldn't he?

I was sweating as I changed into my swim gear. Last session. Last chance to make the team. I was a jerk for even thinking about that with Jeremy in the hospital, but I couldn't help it.

Droid glanced over at me, one eyebrow raised, as I joined the group on deck listening to Coach. Coach kept talking and didn't call me out. I let out a breath, relieved.

"Most of you have probably heard by now, Jeremy Blackburn is in the hospital," Coach said. "I don't have any new information right now. We're all waiting for him to wake up. I'll let you know as soon as I hear anything. Jeremy's part of this team, and we're all rooting for him."

A couple of the Sharks nodded.

"Today is our last practice together," Coach continued. "I know that for those of you who don't make the cut, this will be a difficult time. My door's always open, all right? Now let's do this. For Jeremy."

"For Jeremy," everyone echoed—even the other pond scum, the ones who didn't know him well. I stepped back from the huddle, weirded out.

There wasn't time to think though. Coach set us to work. It was the toughest practice yet—all business, no hazing. Butterfly stroke until my shoulders burned. Red Cap was probably loving it. The Sharks left us alone, maybe because with Jeremy in the hospital it seemed wrong to pull stunts. We just swam.

I worked on my kick when Coach told me to, focusing on technique. Abs tight. Kick from the hip. Back and forth. Flip turn and back again. I wanted to work so I didn't have to think. My times were lousy. No surprise there.

Finally, it was over. Coach's whistle called us out of the water. My arms wobbled as I lifted myself out of the pool.

"Hey—pond scum," Nate said, behind me.

I spun around and pulled off my goggles.

"Don't worry about it," he said. "We all have off days."

I nodded. I wasn't sure what to make of one of the Sharks being nice to me. Was I on the team? Did he know?

He followed me into the locker room. "Coach said you stopped by the hospital. That's cool, you know, that you did that."

I headed for the showers. "Jeremy's a friend."

Steven was waiting for me when I got back to the benches. "Did you hear anything else about the accident?" he asked. "Anything Coach isn't telling us?"

There was something strange about the way he said it. It made me wonder. He and Jeremy weren't exactly friendly, and he had looked pretty pissed off last night. Besides, Jeremy was the one swimmer who consistently edged Steven out of the big races. That had to bug him.

"You know as much as I do," I said carefully. "I didn't get in to see him or anything. It's family only."

He didn't ask me anything else. He just got dressed and headed out.

When I left the locker room, Nate was waiting outside. "Want a ride?" he asked. "Steven's got his wheels." Steven stood beside him, face hidden behind dark sunglasses.

Steven drove a red BMW. Normally I would have given my right arm for the chance to ride in a car like that, but he wasn't exactly on my favorite-people list right now. And it was a bit odd, the way he had come up to me in the locker room. Besides, I had my bike.

But it was a chance to look at his car. If he had hit Jeremy, there would be scratches, or paint missing, or something. Wouldn't there? "Great," I said.

When we reached the car, I made a big show of admiring it. I walked all the way around. There wasn't a scratch. Not on the bumper, not anywhere.

Nate leaned against the door, hands in his pockets, amused. Steven stood straight, arms crossed. Not amused. "Done inspecting my car, officer?" he asked.

I swallowed. After that, I couldn't pretend to suddenly remember that I had brought my bike. I would have to go back for it later. "Just haven't seen it up close before," I said. "Sweet ride." I crammed myself into the backseat. There was lots of room up front for Nate and Steven, but I was eating my kneecaps.

I wiped my palms on my jeans. "So. Tomorrow. Team list, huh?"

"You worried, pond scum?" Steven said, pulling out of the parking space.

Nate laughed. "Play nice," he told Steven. "Seriously, you did great. Except for today. You have nothing to worry about."

"Easy for you to say," I said. "You guys had your turn three years ago."

"Two," Nate said. "I didn't make it the first time I tried out."

That took a minute to process. Sure, Nate wasn't that fast, but I had assumed he joined with the rest of the Sharks. "You didn't—you weren't a swimmer your freshman year?" He hadn't even been on the team when Marcus died. So Nate, at least, had nothing to hide. Maybe he was somebody I could talk to—when Steven wasn't around.

Nate shook his head. "Nope. Speedo boy here was though." He poked Steven's shoulder. In the rearview mirror, I watched Steven scowl.

"Yeah, I figured," I said. I left it at that.

Nate chuckled. "Look, there's a few of us getting together at my place tonight. Parents are away. You in?"

I hesitated, remembering Jeremy's warning about the initiation party. "I haven't even made the team yet," I said. Anyhow, I wasn't exactly in a party mood. Not with Jeremy in the hospital.

"This isn't initiation," Nate said. "Just some guys hanging out."

Steven seemed to be studying me in the rearview mirror. It was hard to tell, with those glasses of his. "Don't know," I said.

"If you want to be part of the team, you have to act like it," Steven said.

Nate nodded. "Life has to go on. Jeremy would have wanted it that way."

They were talking like Jeremy was dead. It got my back up. I met Steven's gaze, as best I could. "I'm sure that's exactly what he'll say," I said. "When he wakes up."

chapter eight

It turned out Droid was going to the party and that most of the pond scum were invited. I was obviously paranoid. Jeremy's comments had rubbed off on me.

"Ask Coach," Droid said, his head in the bathroom sink. He was re-dyeing his hair for the occasion. "He's signed permission for all of us. Thinks it's good for team spirit or. something. Dude, you've got to come.. There'll be girls. I've heard about Nate's parties."

It wasn't unusual for guys to sign out on weekends so they could stay off campus at each other's houses. Not for the ones that lived nearby, anyhow. It just hadn't come up for me before. Like I said, rich-boy clubs.

So Droid, his hair freshly blue, doubled me back to Yale after dinner to pick up my bike. From there, we took our time riding to the address he had written on the back of his hand. Nate lived only a few blocks away from the school. As we got close, music blared. Expensive cars lined the street.

"Why would anyone who lives so close to school need to board?" I asked.

Droid shrugged. "Parents travel, maybe. Who cares? Girls, Bram. Girls."

Sure enough, there were more girls than guys at the party. Inside, the bass was cranked so loud it pounded in my bones. This was a mansion—big rooms, lots of them. The walls were all white, and there were black leather couches. The patio doors opened onto a huge backyard. The air inside was ripe with beer and sweat.

Two girls in miniskirts wandered past, looking us up and down.

Droid grinned and rubbed his hands together.

I lost him after that. At one point I saw Red Cap in the kitchen, talking to a tall girl who totally outclassed him. She looked bored.

Along a hallway was a collection of photos of an older man who looked like Nate. It had to be his dad. In each picture, he was smiling with a different famous person. Singers. Actors. Politicians. Athletes. There was even a picture of him golfing with Coach, back in Coach's younger days. I grinned at that one.

In a room with a giant television, the Sharks were clustered in a corner. "To Jeremy," they said and all took a shot. It pissed me off. What pissed me off even more was that Steven didn't raise his glass to join the toast.

I was about to go over and say something when they moved. At the back of the group was someone small. Someone with blond hair and three silver hoops in each ear.

The air whooshed out of me as if someone had punched me in the gut. Abby, drinking with the Sharks—with *Steven*—while her brother lay in the hospital? What was she trying to prove?

She saw me and waved. "Bram! You came!" She giggled.

I had seen Abby drink exactly once, at an ill-advised birthday party back in Storrs. She was not a giggly drunk. I narrowed my eyes. "What are you doing here?"

"We were just toasting Jeremy. Toasting all about Jeremy." She smiled, looking unfocused. "Want to make a toast?"

"No. And neither do you. We're getting out of here," I said.

Steven stepped forward, arms crossed. "Who put you in charge?"

Nate put a hand on his shoulder. "Relax, buddy. How about we let Abby decide? Abby, what do you want to do?"

I squeezed her hand, hoping she would say the right thing. I didn't want to take on the entire senior swim team to get her back to Wallingford. I looked around, hoping for a glimpse of blue hair. No luck.

She squeezed back. "I'm gonna go," she said thickly. "Got a lot to catch up on, me and Bram. Bye, Jeremy's friends. Nice meeting you."

Steven stepped forward again, but Nate said something to him that I couldn't hear. Whatever it was, it stopped Steven cold.

Abby stumbled a little as we walked away, then, as we headed down the hall and out of sight, she suddenly remembered how to walk again. "Thanks for getting me out of there," she whispered. "I was starting to think I'd be stuck with them all night." Her words were perfectly clear.

I stopped walking. "Abby, what was that back there?"

"Shh. Not here." A couple passed us and she giggled and leaned against me, smelling like oranges. "We should find a room."

"We should—what?" It was suddenly hot in the hallway. I tugged at my collar. "What?"

"You say that a lot. Relax. I'll leave your virtue intact." She eyed me. "It is still intact, isn't it?"

I closed my eyes. This wasn't happening. In a minute I'd open my eyes again, and Droid and I would be arriving at the party.

I opened them. Abby was watching me. Her face had turned red. "Let's just get out of here, okay?" she said.

I tugged my collar again. "Droid. I mean—I came with my roommate."

It took a few minutes for me to locate him, deep in conversation with a dark-haired girl. I signaled that I was leaving. He gave me a thumbs-up. I met Abby out front. The night air had frost in it. Abby shivered, and I gave her my jacket.

"So what was that about?" I asked, pushing my bike. Wallingford was even closer to Nate's house than Strathmore was.

"I thought they might be talking about what happened," she said. "If anyone suspected Coach, I thought I might over-hear something."

"And did you?" She had to see the truth by now. Coach didn't have anything to do with Jeremy's accident.

She shook her head. "Once they found out who I was, everybody just wanted to talk about how great Jeremy is. I think they were trying to make me feel better."

Yeah. Pouring shots into a pretty girl. I'm sure that was exactly what they were trying to do. I squeezed my handlebars. "So you weren't drinking."

She shrugged. "Only what I couldn't dump into the plant."

I thought about that. "Were you this devious when we were dating?"

Abby laughed.

We walked in silence back to Wallingford. It was one of those cold, clear nights where the stars look just out of reach. Finally, we arrived at the tall black iron fence around Wallingford. It had points like spears all along the top. Abby used her pass card to open the gate.

I walked with her as far as her dorm building. Two lion statues, one asleep, one awake, guarded the heavy wooden front doors.

"Here," she said, handing me my jacket. It was warm. She started up the stairs.

"Abby—"

She looked down at me, twisting one of her earrings.

"How's Jeremy?" I blurted.

"The same," she said. She shoved some leaves off the step with the toe of her shoe. "They're keeping him sedated. Mom and Dad think I should stick to my normal routine."

"Undercover work and all," I said.

She smiled. "Something like that."

"I'll go to the hospital with you tomorrow," I said. "If you want."

She hesitated. I held my breath. "That'd be nice," she finally said.

I wasn't glad Jeremy was hurt. I wasn't, not even a little bit. But it was good to be spending time with Abby again. I rode home, thinking about our plan to meet up the next day.

chapter nine

Abby and I biked together to the hospital. I waited outside the ICU while she went in to see Jeremy. Only two visitors were allowed in at a time. Her father came out, and we talked about the weather. "Did you want to go in?" he asked at one point.

I shook my head. Abby probably needed her mom in there more than she needed me. Besides, Jeremy wouldn't even know I was there. "When he's awake," I said. "I'll visit him properly when he wakes up."

Mr. Blackburn nodded. He didn't seem to know what to do with his hands.

I flipped through a four-year-old *Life* magazine and pretended to be interested in one of the articles. Mr. Blackburn looked out a window. Some of the tension went out of his shoulders.

Whoever did this to Jeremy had a lot to answer for.

"Do—" I hesitated to bring it up, but if anyone could tell me what was happening with the investigation, it was Jeremy's dad. "Do the police have any idea who did it?"

He shook his head. "They're investigating."

"He was supposed to meet me that morning," I said. "To go for a run. He didn't show up."

Mr. Blackburn blinked. "Did you tell the police that?"

"No one asked," I said. I promised to give the police a call later. Mr. Blackburn thought it would be best if I went through the headmaster.

Finally, Abby came out, red-eyed. Her dad gave her a hug before he went back in.

Abby and I went for coffee. She put three sugars in hers. She never used to drink coffee. She must have picked it up at Wallingford. "He's stable," she said. "No change, but I don't think there's supposed to be any change yet. By Wednesday, they might start letting him wake up."

"That's good, right?" I asked.

She nodded. Her hands were wrapped around her coffee cup as if she was trying to warm them. "Can you get me into his room?"

I thought about it. Girls weren't allowed upstairs in the dorms, but it still happened. "I can get you into the dorm," I said. "I don't have a key to his room."

She smiled. "I'll pick the lock with my Swiss Army knife." She patted her pocket.

I stared at her. Maybe a little too long, because she laughed.

"Relax, I don't know how to pick locks. Jeremy loses things. He got sick of paying the lost-key penalty, so I keep a spare at my place."

I blew across the top of my coffee. "What do you want in his room?"

"Get me in, and I'll tell you," she said.

She had gone to Nate's party on her own. If she was going to play detective, maybe it was better if I helped her. At least I could try to keep her from doing anything crazy where Coach was concerned.

And I didn't exactly hate spending time with her.

On the way back to school, we passed a wig shop. They had a display of scarves, hats and different-length wigs in the window—even swim caps designed to look like fish. One of them had a giant shark face on it, with fins and everything. I bought it for Droid.

The swim team results were probably posted by now. They hadn't been after breakfast. I needed to check, but I wasn't sure I wanted Abby with me when I did.

Maybe it was stupid, buying a swim cap for Droid when I didn't know if he had made the team. But it felt right.

"It's for good luck," I told Abby.

She nodded. "We could use some of that."

chapter ten

The Sunday after a Saturday-night party was a good time for sneaking a girl into the dorm. Not too many people around. I had to bribe a couple of freshmen playing video games in the common room, who looked up as Abby and I passed by.

Step one was getting her to my room. That was easy. Step two, getting into Jeremy's room without being noticed, was going to be harder. Bribes wouldn't cut it. I needed us to be invisible.

Droid was napping when we got in. He grunted and sat up at the sound of the door, scrubbing at his spiky blue hair with both hands. At least he was wearing a T-shirt. "What is it? Is the list up yet?" When he finally noticed Abby, his eyes widened. "Dude," he said. "That's a girl."

"Keenly observed," I said.

He frowned and looked at Abby again, as if checking that she was still there. "She's hot," he finally said.

"Also, she can hear you," I said.

Behind me, Abby laughed. "We need your help."

Droid rolled onto his back and stared at the glow-in-the-dark stars he had stuck to the ceiling. "It's a computer, isn't it? It's always a computer. Just finished reformatting Andrew's hard drive."

I frowned, not recognizing the name.

"Red Cap," Droid explained.

"Well, computers are kind of your thing," I pointed out. "But actually, it isn't a computer. Not this time."

Droid looked at me. "I'm listening."

We explained we needed a distraction while Abby and I snuck into Jeremy's room. Droid refused to pull the fire alarm. "I could get fined," he said. "Besides, it's unoriginal."

"Unoriginal," Abby said, studying Droid's stars. "Bram, did you show him the swim cap yet?"

Droid's eyes lit up when he saw it. "Now that has potential," he said. "Yes. I can create for you a distraction. It will be a pleasure."

Abby grinned at him. "You said you're good with computers?" she asked. "If Jeremy had something password-protected on his computer, could you open it?"

Droid sighed. "I told you, it's always a computer," he complained to me. He turned back to Abby. "Unless Jeremy's middle name is NASA, I can get you into his system, yes. But I warn you. If he has protected files, there's a ninety-five-percent chance they're porn. Do you really want to know?"

Abby promised to shoulder the burden of knowledge.

Five minutes later, we had a plan. Droid would provide a distraction downstairs. Abby and I would wait a few minutes, then head up to Jeremy's room and look for whatever she needed to look for. While we were there, we would grab his laptop and bring it back to Droid.

Droid tugged off his T-shirt and put on the swim cap. He stood in front of us wearing boxers and a bathing cap.

"Um...Droid?" I was afraid to ask.

"You wanted a distraction," he said. "Tell Jeremy's hot sister to cover her eyes."

I covered mine too. A few seconds later, the door slammed. Droid's boxer shorts were crumpled on the floor. Hoots of laughter came from down the hall.

"I think that's our distraction," I said.

Abby nodded solemnly. "We must honor it. Let's go."

chapter eleven

Anyone who was hanging around for the afternoon ran downstairs when word of the "Shark Streaker" spread. Abby and I made it to Jeremy's room and closed the door behind us. It smelled stale, like home does when you come back from vacation.

As a dorm rep, Jeremy had a single room. It was average messy. Not a pigsty, but the bedspread was rumpled and there were socks on the floor. He had the same Michael Phelps poster I did—from the Beijing Olympics, where Phelps took eight golds.

"Now what?" I asked.

"Now we look around," Abby said. "Look for something that might tell us who was after him." She didn't mention Coach.

"You don't even know what we're here for?"

Abby avoided my gaze. "Listen, something bad happened on the swim team three years ago, and Jeremy had proof," she said. "He was going to come forward with it."

"Marcus Tam," I said, remembering what Jeremy had told me in the weight room.

Abby's eyebrows shot up. "Yeah, it was about Marcus. What do you know?"

What did I know? Nothing that would lead anybody to plow into Jeremy with a car. "That the team covered up the hazing part of it. That Jeremy...I think he feels responsible."

She nodded.

"But, Abby, that still doesn't mean Jeremy's accident had anything to do with Marcus. Did you mention this to the police?"

She dropped into Jeremy's desk chair. "I told my parents, and Dad blew up at me. He doesn't want to believe anyone would hurt Jeremy on purpose. I tried the police, and they pretty much patted me on the head. They think it might have been a drunk driver."

She was trying not to make a big deal of it, but her voice shook when she got to the head-patting part. The surest way to piss Abby off: treat her like a little kid. "I promise not to blow up at you. Or to pat you on the head," I said.

She took a deep breath. "If I find the proof and bring it to the police, they will have to listen to me. Think about it. Coach had a lot to lose if the truth got out."

I wasn't so sure. "Marcus Tam—that was three years ago. The police must have investigated it then. If anything was wrong, it would have come out. Jeremy was going to prove it was hazing. So what? It's in the past. Marcus Tam has been dealt with.

You have to think about other possibilities. What if Jeremy's hit-and-run really was just an accident?"

Her eyes narrowed. "You don't believe that."

"No," I said. "But I'm thinking about who benefits with Jeremy out of the picture. It's not Coach. He's lost one of his best swimmers. What about Steven? They're seniors now, and Steven's been eating Jeremy's wake for years. Jeremy can't race now, and suddenly Steven's our top-ranked swimmer. Not a bad place to be, especially with college applications due."

"You think this was about *swimming*?"

I crossed my arms. "Swimming is important." A poster of Michael Phelps was on the wall. How could she talk like that in front of him?

"You don't kill somebody over swimming," she said.

"You and I don't," I said. "Does Steven strike you as a balanced individual?"

"Just because you don't like him doesn't make him the bad guy," Abby said.

"And just because you want to believe in Coach doesn't mean he's innocent. All I'm saying is, we have to work with the facts."

"Right," I said, looking around Jeremy's room. "So let's find the facts. Where does Jeremy keep his laptop? You wanted Droid to take a look at it."

She frowned. The desk was empty. "I'd have thought..." She spun around in the chair. "I don't know."

We looked in every place a laptop might reasonably be stored. In the closet. In backpacks. And in places that made no sense at all, like in drawers and under Jeremy's pillow. "He wasn't out for a run," Abby said, looking in his closet.

"Huh?" I looked up from under the bed.

"His good sneakers. They're still here," Abby said. "He wore these to run in. His old ones are for the rest of the time. Those are the ones he must have had on."

"You didn't see what shoes he was wearing?"

She shook her head. "The police kept his clothes. Evidence."

I sat up on the bed. The carpet had a worn patch, over by the desk chair. I cleared my throat. "He was supposed to meet me," I said, finally looking up at Abby. "At six. He would have had his running shoes on for that." A serious athlete like Jeremy wasn't likely to risk injury over anything as stupid as wearing the wrong shoes.

"So wherever he was going when he got hit by the car, he thought he would have time to come back and change."

Maybe. Or he had changed his mind about the run and didn't bother to let me know. But the run had been his idea. "The night before the accident, I think he wanted to tell me something," I said. I explained how Steven and Nate had interrupted us in the weight room.

"Maybe he was going to show you his proof," Abby said.

I shrugged. There was no way of knowing. Not until Jeremy woke up. "What about his cell phone?" I asked. "Do the police have that too?" Maybe someone called him, or he had called someone. Maybe that would give us a clue.

Abby shook her head. "It wasn't found."

"I don't see it around here, do you?" I slid open the top drawer of his desk. For somebody who lost his keys all the time, Jeremy seemed very organized. The drawer was full of plastic bins with labels. Pens. Pencils. Erasers. Calculator. Flash drives.

Abby laughed. "I gave him those bins, as a joke. He was always borrowing my stuff because he couldn't find his. I'm surprised he actually uses them."

I wasn't sure how well he used them. There were pens in the ruler bin and an eraser in the bin for flash drives. I didn't see any flash drives at all. I had a few of them. Thumb-sized backup, about the size of Abby's tiny Swiss Army knife. Droid and his friends used theirs for swapping movies and software around. "No laptop. No backup drives. Does that seem weird to you? Like maybe he hid all his computer stuff?" I asked

"Or somebody took it," Abby said slowly.

I closed the drawer. "Who else would have a key?"

"A teacher could get in, I bet," she said. "Coach could."

I dropped my head into my hands. She was back on Coach again. It didn't fit. He hadn't even been at the party. But somebody—either Jeremy or whoever had taken his laptop—thought there was something in Jeremy's files worth hiding. His computer, his flash drives, even his phone were missing. It was too much of a coincidence. We needed that laptop.

"I'm going to try and check Steven's room," I said. "I'll get in. Trust me, okay? The computer might be there, or there might be something else there that can point us in the right direction. Just...lay off Coach in the meantime."

Abby studied me. "I'm going to suggest to Mom and Dad that they collect Jeremy's laptop. Just for safekeeping, while he's in the hospital. That way, they'll find out it's missing and tell the police. Okay?"

"Okay," I said. Something occurred to me. "Wouldn't the police already have come in here, looking for his phone?"

Abby shrugged. "Nobody said anything to me about a missing laptop. That's all I know."

I hesitated. I didn't want to fight with her. "Abby—what do you really think we're looking for? What kind of proof are we talking about?"

"Photos," she said. "Proof that Marcus died because of hazing. Proof that Coach Gordon was there."

chapter twelve

After we snuck Abby out, Droid and I raced to Coach's office—the one in the main building, not the one by the swimming pool. Coach was nowhere in sight. The door was closed, and a typewritten page was taped to it. At the top it said: *Swim Team Roster*. Red Cap was reading it. As we drew near, he turned away, a smile on his face. He raised a hand to Droid and I, as if we were his fan club, there to cheer him on.

Droid gave him a halfhearted high five. I was already staring at the list.

Bram Walters. My name was there, under the sophomore category. Droid's wasn't. But of course—his real name wasn't Droid. It was Danilo. Danilo Martinez. I scanned the list again.

Droid wasn't on it.

I backed away. Droid's eyes met mine. His chin was stuck high, his eyes too bright.

My mouth tasted like sawdust. We had both worked so hard. "Droid, man."

"Hey, dude. It's all right. Congratulations," he said. "You deserve the spot."

I smiled, but there was a sinking feeling in my chest. "It wasn't supposed to be just one of us."

Droid shrugged, but it was too casual. It looked forced. "You'd better get going," he said. "Coach wants to see you all at nine o'clock. See? It's there, on the bottom. Poolside meeting. Probably one of his famous pep talks." He made finger quotes around "pep talks."

"Droid—"

He shrugged again. "Catch you back at the room."

I headed to the pool on my own.

I spent Monday morning swim practice thinking over my plan. I wanted to get a look in Steven's room. So as I backstroked through the water, staring at the ceiling, I reviewed the facts.

Someone had gotten into Jeremy's room. And from what the police had said when Abby's parents called them, there wasn't a lot of hope of finding out who. They weren't even sure it was directly related to the hit-and-run. Someone might have taken advantage of the fact that Jeremy was in the hospital, they said. Someone might have grabbed the chance to steal his laptop.

If the missing laptop had done one thing, it had convinced me that Abby was onto something. An accidental hit-and-run? Maybe. An accidental hit-and-run followed

73

by the victim's room being robbed? It didn't take a rocket scientist to see something was off.

Abby was right. Coach could have gotten access to Jeremy's room. But as head boy, it wouldn't have been hard for Steven to come up with a reason to visit the dorm office either. And that was where the spare keys were kept. So Steven also could have done it.

End of lane. Racing turn. My recovery was too slow.

Maybe Jeremy had hidden the laptop himself. But where? If he had hidden it, he must have thought something could go wrong. So he would have put it where someone, either his parents, Abby or me could find it.

But where?

Water rushed past me. I had an outside lane, not the greatest. Outside lanes are slow. You feel the wake more. I could tell by the push of the water that someone was ahead of me—I was fighting somebody else's waves.

If Abby was right and this all tied into Marcus Tam's death and whatever proof Jeremy had, stealing the computer made sense. But what if it wasn't that? What if I was right, and Steven was behind it? What could be on Jeremy's laptop that Steven didn't want anyone to see?

Maybe Steven had sent Jeremy emails. Threats. Maybe he had tried to warn Jeremy off the team.

Maybe the computer, and Jeremy's phone, had to do with whatever had gotten him out of bed in the middle of the night. Maybe he had been going to meet somebody. Maybe he had been on his way to meet whoever ran into him with their car.

Down and up again, dolphin kick. Break the surface and go.

I pulled harder. My body shot through the water. That's the best part of front crawl—when your body feels it was made to move through water. I wasn't fighting anyone's wake now. I focused. *Swim.* Almost there.

End of lane. I hit the wall. Surfaced.

Practice ended. Coach called us over. Our first meet was still more than a month away, so there was plenty of time to decide who would compete in what event, he said. He had a good feeling about this year. If we played our cards right and stayed strong, we had a shot at the state-wide championship. He looked at Steven when he said this.

I was halfway out of the pool area before he finished talking. The other guys made for the showers. I went straight to the locker room. Steven's varsity jacket hung on the hook at the end of the aisle.

I swiped his keys out of his pocket, then dressed faster than I ever had before, yanking my pants up over wet legs. I ran out the door.

I reeked of chlorine, but I had the keys.

I nodded hello to the two boys I met on the way to Steven's room. My hair was dripping. Steven had five keys on his keychain. One was the key to his BMW.

I let myself what-if about that one for half a second before I got back to the business of unlocking his door.

The room was scary neat. Hotel-room neat. As head boy, Steven had no roommate, but even so, shouldn't there have been socks and sweatpants lying around? The room was perfectly clean. The burgundy bedspread looked like it had been ironed into place, and even the pillowcase was smooth. There was a spiral-bound notebook on his desk alongside his computer. Nothing else. Everything was lined up at right angles to the edge of the desk. The chair was pushed in. Books were lined up on shelves according to size. There were no pictures of friends thumb-tacked to the bulletin board, just a class schedule, a school calendar and a swim-team roster. No posters.

The room even smelled kind of bleachy, as if someone had used cleaning products in it recently. I shivered.

I closed the door behind me. It was risky. I wouldn't know if Steven was coming, and I couldn't get out easily. But that was better than someone seeing me in Steven's room and telling him about it.

If Jeremy's laptop was here, it wasn't in plain sight. I checked under the bed. Nothing, not even a dust bunny on the hardwood floor. I started my search. The desk drawers were compulsively organized. And when I got to the closet, I shivered again. The blazers were on the left, all facing the same way. The shirts were next, arranged by color. Then the pants. They were arranged by color too. Everything was lined up. There was nothing wrong with a clean room, but this? This creeped me out. Even Mom wasn't this organized.

I exhaled. How long had I been here? I had to get out before Steven got his hands on a spare key. I moved to the door and listened, making sure there were no footsteps in the hall when I opened the door.

I made it as far as the stairs before I met Steven. He held a set of spare room keys from the front desk, complete with a large, orange keychain. His real keys were heavy in my pocket. I made a fist around them. I would have to find a place to ditch them outside, somewhere between the pool and the main building when no one was looking.

I nodded as we passed. "Good practice."

He nodded back but stopped walking. His eyes narrowed. I felt his stare as I continued down the stairs.

chapter thirteen

I texted Abby that evening to tell her I hadn't found anything in Steven's room. She was going to visit Jeremy after school, so we wouldn't have a chance to talk. Droid and I spent the time after study hall blowing each other up in an online game. He kicked my butt as usual. Maybe it would make him feel better about not making the swim team.

Tuesday after school, Abby texted me to meet her out front and bring my bike. I didn't bother to hide my grin.

"Girl Sherlock?" Droid asked.

I nodded. Maybe we would go for coffee.

Steven wasn't hiding Jeremy's computer in his room. But that didn't mean he wasn't hiding it. And the way the room had been—it didn't seem like a healthy kid's room to me. If Steven felt Jeremy was disordering his universe, he could have done anything to him.

By the time I signed out and made it to the front of the school, she was already riding her bike back and forth along the sidewalk. Her helmet was the same blue as her jeans. A part of me had hoped for the kilt-and-kneesocks-on-a-bicycle thing.

"Let's go—5485 Briarwood," she said. She started riding away, heading north along the street.

"Or in English, hello," I called after her.

So this wasn't a coffee date. Or even a social call. My feet felt heavier all of a sudden.

I caught up with her before we reached the main road. "Where are we going?" I asked. There was no traffic here, so we could ride side by side.

"Your coach's house," she said.

"Oh." I thought about that for a minute. It didn't add up to anything good. "Why?"

"To see what color car his wife drives." She glanced at me, then powered ahead before I could ask questions.

She was upset about Jeremy. I got that. But stalking the coach's wife didn't strike me as a good idea.

Maybe the best thing was to let her get it out of her system. Then we could go for coffee, talk, whatever. At least I was here with her.

After twenty minutes of hard riding, we reached a neighborhood with street names like Birchwood and Oakcliff. It was one of the older parts of New Haven, with big pastel-colored houses and old-fashioned windows. The trees on the boulevard reached across the street, and the leaves were raked into fancy jack-o'-lantern garbage bags. There were a few rental houses too. You could tell those by the patchy lawns and the flags in the windows. Yale students, probably.

The coach's house was a pale yellow two-story with a wide porch. Abby rode past without stopping. I braked just before the driveway. The coach's car—a gray Jetta—wasn't in the driveway, but there was a pale blue Impala there. "This one!" I called.

She wheeled around and glared at me. "Keep riding!"

I rolled my eyes. It was nearly dinnertime. What were the chances of anyone looking out the front windows? But she kept riding, so I followed. She stopped at the drugstore on the corner.

I caught up with her. "Sorry. Didn't realize it was such a stealth mission. Should we have been in disguise?" I smiled, hoping for a laugh.

Her face flushed red. "Forget it." She turned away and wiped her eyes.

I felt like a worm. "Look, I'm sorry. I just—do you want to tell me what's going on here? Because I'm confused."

"The police told Dad it was a dark green car," she said, studying the sidewalk.

"They're going to go public with the information tomorrow."

"A dark green—oh." The pieces clunked into place. "But why did you think Coach's wife had anything to do with it?"

"Not her, dummy, him!" She glared at me.

My jaw dropped so hard that the bike helmet strap dug into my chin. "I told you, he didn't do it."

She looked away. "I thought if you saw the car..."

I took a deep breath and tried again. "You have to understand, I know Coach. He's not the guy. And the cars aren't even the right color, so that proves it, right?"

"It doesn't prove anything," she muttered.

I leaned on the wall of the drugstore and let my head clunk against the brick. My helmet got there first. "Abby, you can't just go chasing after people. This is for the police to solve."

"I thought you cared about Jeremy."

"I do, but the police will handle it. Look, I'm a swimmer. You want to talk front crawl, I'm your guy. I'm not a detective, and neither are you."

She crossed her arms and looked away.

"Why don't we go for coffee? We can talk about this, okay?" We would be late for dinner, but so what?

Abby studied me for long enough that I started to feel fidgety. I held myself still.

"See you around, Bram," she said. She kicked her bicycle into motion.

Panic rolled in my stomach. "Wait!" I pedaled hard and caught up with her as she turned onto a side street. I pulled ahead, then yanked my bike crossways in front of her, cutting her off.

She braked, but not fast enough. We crashed down together, and I scraped across the asphalt. We lay there, panting, in a tangle of limbs and bicycles. My right leg and arm burned.

"What the hell was that?" she shouted, shoving me.

"Are you okay?" I was an idiot. I was the world's biggest idiot.

"No thanks to you." Slowly, she stood and brushed gravel off her jeans. One knee was torn. Red, broken skin showed underneath. Her cycling gloves had protected her hands. She was moving fine. I exhaled.

"I never meant to—I just wanted to talk," I said.

"Nothing to talk about," she said, glaring. "You don't want to help, fine. Just stay out of my way."

"Abby, I—" But she was already pulling her bike free from mine. She checked it over, making sure nothing was bent or broken.

She wasn't interested in me. She never had been. I was only useful.

"Are you okay? Can you stand?" she asked. Her voice was cold. It didn't match the words.

"Fine," I said.

I watched her ride away.

chapter fourteen

I made it back to school just in time for Tuesday chicken dinner. I didn't say much, not even when Droid asked about my torn sleeve and the scrapes on my arm.

And when I finished eating, I was still fuming. If I were a cartoon character, there would have been a black cloud over my head.

"Study hall, bro?" Droid asked on the way up to our room. I grunted and shook my head. I wasn't going to be able to concentrate, math test or no math test.

Instead, I changed into a pair of long shorts and a T-shirt. The T-shirt sleeve flapped against the road rash on my arm. Each touch stung. It felt sharp. I wanted that. "I'll be in the weight room," I told Droid.

He raised a thick eyebrow. Yeah, I'd been for a bike ride. But I needed to move, and no way would I be allowed off campus for a run at this time of night.

The weight room was deserted. Good. Somebody had strung a row of cardboard skeletons along the wall of mirrors. Somebody else had taken a marker and labeled the bones. The room smelled like stale sweat, as usual.

I started on the treadmill. It wasn't the same as a real run. But at least my feet were pounding, my blood was racing and I didn't have to think.

My legs felt rubbery. After the treadmill, I moved on to my upper-body workout. One of the fluorescent lights in the room was loose and buzzing. It set my teeth on edge.

The last time I'd been in this room, Jeremy had been here too. I took a second to hope with every fiber in my body that he was going to get better.

And then I worked. Arms out, then back slowly, pushing from the shoulders. Ten presses. A break. Ten more. I knew my routine by heart. Sweat dripped into my eyes and stung. Jeremy would have said I was pressing too much weight. I didn't care. I wanted to.

Every time Abby slipped into my thoughts, I drove her out of my mind. I had just been...convenient for her. Someone to help her find answers.

Hell, if Jeremy was my brother, I would probably have done the same. He was a friend. And he had taken a big risk, telling me as much as he had.

Was what happened to him my fault?

I stood slowly. My knees shook. I looked around the room, and suddenly none of the machines made sense. Wires and pulleys, weights and benches. Everything became tangled up together. I didn't know where I was in my routine or what came next. I stared back at myself in the mirror. Sweaty hair. Scraped-up arm.

Guilty conscience.

I shook my head, trying to focus. What happened to Jeremy was the fault of whoever had done it. Steven. Coach. I didn't even know anymore. And maybe we would never find out.

Stupid Jeremy and his hiding games. Talking in riddles, never coming right out and telling me or Abby what information he had or why it mattered. Or where he hid it.

The fluorescent light stopped buzzing. All of a sudden the room felt very still. What if Jeremy *had* told me where he hid it? The night Steven and Nate had been here. He hadn't had the chance to talk openly. Did he know then that something might happen to him?

I tried to remember his words. I sat down and replayed the scene in my head. He had been on his way out, and Steven and Nate were right behind him. I'd been pissed off at him. What had he said on my way back inside? Something about smaller weights making a difference.

That was no help. He was just repeating the advice he had given me earlier.

But there was something about the way he said it.

What if he had already hidden the pictures, or laptop, or flash drive or whatever it was, before Steven and Nate arrived? Or what if something had happened, when Steven and Nate were talking to him, to make him decide to return and hide them the morning before our run? He would have had a hiding place picked out. And maybe he wanted to give me a clue.

Less weight.

I scanned the room. It was hard to know where to look without knowing what I was looking for. It couldn't be a laptop. That was too big. A flash drive was small though. Or a photo.

The smallest weights in the room were the free weights. I picked one off the top shelf. Three pounds. Not big enough to be used very often. I shook it. If Jeremy had pried off the rubber tip on the end, a flash drive might fit inside the metal bar. Nothing rattled. I tried the other weights on the top shelf.

Maybe the free weights were too complicated a hiding place. I was using the leg press when he made the first comment about weight. The leg-press weights were long, flat rectangles stacked on top of each other. They sat on my right-hand side when I was using the press, and they moved up and down with the pulley. Jeremy had moved the pin up from where I usually kept it. What number? What weight had he picked?

I sat on the leg-press bench and put the pin at the lightest weight setting—the top one. I pushed out with my legs and watched the weight fly up beside me. Nothing underneath that one.

Weight down. Move the pin. Next setting. Nothing.

I kept going until I was pressing 160. Close to my body weight. Lifting it and twisting to the right to grope under the raised weight was a lot harder than lifting with proper form. It was getting tough to hold the weight while I reached underneath. The bottom of the stack of weights was lower and heavier each time.

I pushed my legs out and locked my knees in place, then twisted my body to the right. I patted the underside of the weight, fingers flinching in and out.

There was something there. Something flat and smooth. I found a corner of tape and picked at it until I pulled away a photo taped under the weight.

My legs shook. I lowered the weight and looked at the picture.

It was of the Sharks. Most of them anyhow. Younger by a few years, but recognizable. They were wearing boxers and had been sprayed with shaving cream or something. They stood beside a glass table with a bunch of shot glasses in front of them. Some kind of drinking game. Steven's eyes were half closed, and one guy looked totally plastered. He had dark hair and he might have been Asian. It had to be Marcus, Jeremy's roommate. There were other guys, fully dressed, standing around and cheering. Those must have been the senior swimmers back then.

Coach was in the picture too, holding up some kind of a large funnel. Marcus was drinking out of it while Coach poured beer in the top. Coach.

And later that night, Marcus died of alcohol poisoning.

chapter fifteen

Droid looked up from his computer as I entered the room. "Dude, you reek."

"Sorry." I usually showered before I came back. Tonight I hadn't wanted to risk letting the photo out of my sight, even for a second. I had hidden it under my shirt on the way up the stairs.

I walked past Droid and sat on the edge of my bed to stare at the picture again.

"You okay?" Droid asked.

I glanced up. He had turned around in his desk chair to face me. "Huh? Yeah," I said. My thoughts tumbled. Jeremy. Abby. Coach. "I found this. I think it's from Jeremy."

"Pass it here, bro."

I turned it facedown on my bed.

"I'm not going to hurt it," he said.

"It's not that." Whoever was after this had wanted it badly enough to hurt Jeremy. That meant anyone who saw it was in danger. "You sure you want to be part of this?"

"Does a Shark piss in the water?" He held out his hand.

I handed him the picture.

He studied it, then whistled. "Serious stuff."

"I know."

"This could end Coach's career."

"I know."

"What are you going to do?"

I shrugged. My head ached. I hadn't wanted to believe Coach was at the party. I hadn't wanted to believe he was hiding anything.

Did this mean he had tried to kill Jeremy to save his reputation? Was that why he had been at the hospital that morning, to finish Jeremy off if he got the chance?

No. It didn't fit.

"At least let me scan it," Droid said. "You need some kind of backup."

"I don't know," I said. "It seems to me that keeping a copy of this picture isn't good for one's life expectancy." I tried for a light tone, but missed.

Droid waved at his computer. "Please. If I hide something in here, it stays hidden. No one will ever know it exists."

"Not unless their middle name is NASA, right?"

He grinned. "Exactly."

"This still doesn't mean Coach did it," I said. "It proves that he was at that party, and that he messed up. But it doesn't mean he tried to kill Jeremy." I couldn't pretend the two things were unrelated anymore. But Coach wasn't the one I saw talking to Jeremy the night before he almost died. It had been Steven and Nate. Maybe Steven wanted Coach in his debt. Maybe he wanted the picture so he could blackmail Coach with it, to get that starting spot.

"Dude. It's not your problem. You have to take it to the police."

I shook my head. "The minute I do that, Coach's career is over. You said it yourself. And it might be for nothing. They're looking for a green car. Coach doesn't even have a green car."

Droid bit his lip. He looked up at his Mexican flag.

"Promise me you won't go behind my back," I said. "Just give me a chance to figure out what to do. Okay?"

He promised. But he didn't look happy about it.

chapter sixteen

I lay in bed, staring at hairline cracks in the ceiling. Droid was asleep. I had taped the picture to the wall behind my Michael Phelps poster, but I saw it every time I closed my eyes.

It would ruin Coach's career, no question. He had been at a party where underage students were drinking. Students he was directly responsible for, as a coach and a faculty member. And one of those boys had died later that night. The press would barbecue him.

I punched my pillow into a different shape. How had the Sharks all worked out their cover story? There must have been some kind of investigation. Had the Sharks all agreed to lie to protect Coach? Had some of them, maybe Jeremy, been forced into it somehow?

The room was too hot. I kicked off my covers and stared at the ceiling again.

My cell phone rang. I jumped to grab it. "H'lo?" my voice croaked.

"Hey," Abby said.

It was late. According to the glowing red numbers on the clock, it was 1:26. My pulse pounded. "Is he all right?" I asked.

There was a pause. "Oh," she finally said. "You thought—no. Jeremy's fine. No change, but they'll try letting him wake up tomorrow. We'll know more then."

My hands were clammy. I pinned the phone against my shoulder and wiped them on my bedspread. "That's good, right?"

"It's good," she said. "Probably. Sorry for scaring you."

I felt what had to be a big stupid smile spread across my face. Jeremy was okay. She had called anyhow. "Sorry for crashing into you," I said.

She laughed, low and quiet. Something tightened inside my chest.

"I forgive you," she said. "But my bike is still holding a grudge."

"I'll stay away from your bike then," I said. "Nothing worse than a bike with a grudge."

Across the room, Droid mumbled something and rolled over in his sleep.

We were quiet then, Abby and I. Maybe each waiting for the other to say something. Now was my chance to tell her about the picture. If I waited any longer, it would be too late.

"Bram—"

"Abby, I—" I started.

"Go ahead," she said.

I shook my head. "No. You first."

"I just wanted to say, it's not all about Jeremy," she said. "I mean, it is. He's all I'm thinking about right now. But...I would want to hang out with you anyway. You just have to be patient, okay?"

It wasn't the time to tell her about the photo. I didn't want to fight with her about turning Coach in.

"Okay," I said.

chapter seventeen

Wednesdays, we had classes in the morning, sports in the afternoon. I'd had trouble sleeping the night before, so I dozed off after lunch and woke in time to rush to the pool. The other guys were already there, standing in a pack around Coach. I made my way to the back of the group. Water lapped at the sides of the pool and threw squiggly reflections up on the ceiling.

Coach made a mark on the sheet and winked at me. "Okay, boys, let's see what you've got. Front crawl, ten lengths to warm up. Nice and steady. Go."

Like always, the Sharks were first in the water. We lined up behind them, pacing ourselves a few body lengths apart. As recently graduated pond scum, and because I had been late to the pool, I was one of the last in line, just behind Red Cap. The tile floor was dry and gripped my bare feet. It only felt like that when the pool had been empty for a while.

My turn. My toes grabbed the rounded edge of the pool. I dove in, shallow and easy, then broke into a measured, even front crawl, pacing myself to the rest of the group.

The pace was too slow for me. I wanted to work harder, to push ahead. I forced myself to keep it steady and to focus on form. But thoughts kept creeping into my head.

Steven wasn't likely to tell me anything. But what about the other Sharks? What if I asked one of them about the party Marcus was at three years ago? Nothing that would scare anyone off, just a little prodding. I could pretend I was nervous because of our own upcoming party.

Which Shark though? I ran through them in my head. Most of them did whatever Steven asked. And Nate hadn't even made the team that year.

But maybe he had heard rumors. He had less at stake than the others.

At the wall, I dove under and turned.

I had my plan.

After practice, I waited around for Nate outside the athletics building. He had his hands in his pockets, and he raised one eyebrow when he saw me. "Don't tell me you want backstroke pointers."

I grinned and fell in beside him. "I wanted to ask you about the initiation party," I said. "Someone said it was at your house."

"Unlikely," he said. "I'm not sure who's hosting this year. Whoever's parents go away first, right?"

"Ha." I scuffed fallen leaves with my sneakers, trying to work out how to lead the conversation where I needed it to go. "So who shows at these things? Do we bring dates?"

"Pond scum don't," he said. "Not unless you want your dates to see you...well, let's just say you probably don't want that." His turn to grin.

"Ah. You fill me with confidence. So, will Coach be there? Is it best behavior until he leaves, or what?"

Nate shook his head. "Coach is cool. He'll show, but he won't stay long."

"Is that what happened at the party three years ago?" I asked.

Nate stopped walking. I winced. Too blunt.

"Who told you about that?" he asked.

"The guys." I shrugged. "I was just wondering if Coach was there."

Nate straightened. I'm not exactly short, but he towered over me. He took his hands out of his pockets and didn't look so easygoing anymore. "You don't want to go asking questions about what happened that night."

Something in my face must have worried him. He let out a phony-sounding laugh and clapped me on the back. "Relax. It's just, no point digging up bad memories, right? Anyhow, Coach wasn't there. Not by the time things got going."

"Right," I said. So Nate didn't know. Maybe it was time he did. I studied him, deciding whether to trust him. "What if he was though? What if I have proof?"

Nate's eyes lingered on my face. "Then, for the good of the team, I suggest you lose it."

chapter eighteen

Abby and I had plans to meet for a run after she finished school. I had the photo with me, tucked into the pocket of my windbreaker. It wasn't too late, not really. I had only found out last night. I could say I hadn't wanted to upset her in the middle of the night. She would forgive that.

So why was I nervous?

I paced outside Wallingford as I waited, then leaned on the iron fence bars and stretched my calves.

Abby finally appeared, wearing a tight-fitting black hoodie. Any other time, I might have stopped to appreciate it.

We started off at a light jog. "How's Jeremy doing?" I asked. The edge of the picture prodded my stomach.

"He's slow to wake up," she said. "But they say that could be a good thing. Like his body's just taking the time it needs, you know? Mom promised to call me if there was any change." She tripped over a bump where the sidewalk squares didn't meet up properly. "Want to go to the road?"

"Sure." The roads around Wallingford and Strathmore were pretty quiet. Not a lot of traffic, even at this time of day, when people were coming home from work and school. Road running was better for the shins anyhow.

I tried to work out a way to bring up the picture. I needed to come clean, but also make her see reason. We would wait and see what happened with Jeremy, and let the police figure out who had been behind the hit-and-run. If it was Coach, then yeah, we would produce the picture, because it mattered. But if Jeremy's accident was just some random hit-and-run, or if it was Steven, there was no point destroying Coach's life over a mistake he made three years ago.

We passed Nate's house, where the party had been, just as a dark-green Mercedes pulled out of the driveway. I nudged Abby's arm. Despite the tinted windows, we were close enough to see inside the car.

A tall man was driving. Nate's dad— I recognized him from the pictures. He waved us to go ahead.

"Come on," Abby said. She smiled at him as we jogged past the driveway. I followed her, stiffly. My knees seemed to have forgotten what to do.

The car turned left and passed us. I kept my eyes on Abby. We were on the shady side of the street, but I was pretty sure that had nothing to do with the goose bumps on my arms. "A green car," I said.

"Just keep jogging," she said. "Act like nothing's wrong."

But the green car was a link to the swim team and Jeremy's accident.

"Are you going to tell the police?" I asked.

"What, so they can pat me on the head again?" She frowned. "We don't know that it's the same car."

I took a deep breath. "There's something I have to give you," I said.

chapter nineteen

The following day we had no official practice, but Coach usually opened the pool early Tuesdays and Thursdays so we could fit in a before-breakfast swim if we wanted. Today was Thursday. And man, did I need the pool time. I hoped it would be quiet.

Droid was still sleeping when I made my way across the dark, still grounds. Frosty grass crunched under my sneakers, and my breath fogged the air.

A couple of Sharks were there before me. Not Steven, not Nate. Coach was in his poolside office, doing something on the computer. He nodded when one of the Sharks spoke to him, but he seemed distracted. I didn't speak to anyone, just nodded hello and got ready to swim.

Abby had the picture. She had promised not to do anything with it until we decided on a plan together.

I got a lane to myself so I could set my own pace and swim slow, focusing on kick form, or swim fast, just for the feel of cutting through the water. I liked the rush of water past my ears, the smell of chlorine. I liked the reach and follow-through as I pulled myself forward. I liked the pattern of my breathing every fifth stroke, and the way the water held me up just a little, just enough.

When I was in the water, things made sense.

I swam until the other guys started getting out of the pool. The clock read *7:30*. Time to go, if I wanted a decent breakfast.

I dragged myself up on the ladder. My legs shook. Maybe I'd overdone it the past few days. I took a moment on the pool deck to stretch. It was rare, having the place to myself like this.

Stretching felt good. So good that I headed into the sauna. I could rush breakfast. I sat sideways along the lowest bench and peeled off my cap and goggles, letting the heat soak into my muscles. I leaned forward to grab my ankles, bending at the waist, feeling the pull along the back of my legs. Good. I closed my eyes, starting to count to thirty. It smelled of warm cedar and something metallic. And it was quiet.

Then the door rattled. I jerked my head up, but the door stayed closed.

I tried to relax into my stretch again, but something felt wrong. I swung my feet off the bench and onto the already-dry tile floor. I reached for the door.

It stuck.

I pushed again, turning the handle as far as it would go. The handle moved freely, but something was jamming the door.

The outside lock was fastened. I tried again. Suddenly the air felt a thousand times hotter. There was no temperature control inside. I shoved at the door, throwing my shoulder into it. Nothing. I wasn't going to be able to open it myself.

I sat on the bench. This was a joke. It had to be. I took deep breaths. Tried to make myself relax. Then, after a few minutes had passed, I tried again. Nothing.

Blood pounded in my ears. Someone had locked me in. One of the Sharks— it had to be. I pounded at the narrow glass window, but there was no sign of anyone else on the pool deck. Not that I could see. I wanted to believe it was a joke, but after what happened to Jeremy, I couldn't be sure.

"Let me out!" I shouted, slamming against the door again. It didn't budge. I banged on the window. "Coach! Are you there? Let me out!"

Moving in the heat made me dizzy. It was hard to breathe. The air scorched my throat. I dropped onto the bench, head in my hands. Forced myself to think, to breathe slowly. There had to be a way out. The door was stuck, but the window—could I break the glass? Once the window was broken, I could reach through it and unlock the door.

A sliced arm was better than death by pressure cooker. At least I'd be free.

I stood, tensed my body, aimed my shoulder at the glass window and slammed into it.

Nothing.

I drew back, tried again. And again. My shoulder throbbed. I squeezed my eyes shut, leaned my head against the hot glass and pounded at the door with the heel of my left hand. "Someone. Please. Let me out."

I made myself think. I needed to break the glass. Slamming my shoulder against the window hadn't worked. There was no room in the tiny sauna for a running start. I needed a smaller point of impact. More force in less space.

I turned, slowly. The wooden benches sat behind me, three rows of them, each higher than the one in front, like seating in a stadium. From the back wall to the door was maybe six or eight feet. If I jumped...

This was going to hurt.

I climbed onto the second bench. From there, I had a good chance of hitting the window with my outstretched hand. I pulled in a deep breath that burned all the way down, then coughed the hot air out and breathed in again with my hand covering my mouth and nose. My face, my hands, every part of me was slippery with sweat. Salt dripped into my eyes.

I wiped my right arm on the wooden bench behind me, then changed my mind and decided to use the left, instead. The hand I didn't write with. I wiped it on the bench, trying to get the sweat off so I wouldn't slide off the glass.

There's a moment, before you dive into the pool. Your body is ready. You're in position, ready to dive. But there's a split second, when the starting gun sounds, when you could dive or not. A good swimmer trains past that point, so it's not a conscious thing, diving into the water. It's instinct.

I had no instinct for diving into a door.

I aimed, stretched my left arm out, made a fist and jumped.

chapter twenty

The force of my crash echoed up my arm. Glass shattered. My body slammed against the door. My left cheekbone smashed the window frame, and my arm hung through the broken window. For a split second there was no pain, no blood. Only silence, and my heartbeat in my ears.

Then I heard glass fall and felt the pain.

My knuckles throbbed. Deep cuts burned along my arm. Blood welled up, then started to pour from a gouge along the inside of my forearm. I felt dizzy. My vision narrowed. All I could see was the blood on my skin and a darkness closing in from the sides.

I swallowed. Breathed. Pushed back the darkness. I was on my knees, inside the sauna, clutching my left arm. It hurt.

I stood shakily, leaning against the door. My right hand was slippery with blood from holding my left forearm. I forced myself to let go, to reach through the broken window, to feel for the lock. Somehow, I opened the door. Cool air.

I staggered three steps, just enough to get clear of the glass. There was a first-aid kit on the wall somewhere.

I couldn't remember where. The pool deck spun.

Then Coach was there. "Bram? What—?" He was beside me, kneeling. He grabbed my arm. Something sharp cut me and I screamed. He swam back and forth in front of my eyes, like we were underwater.

"Take a deep breath. We'll get you fixed up. Bram. Bram, look at me." He slapped my face. "Hold this." He had a towel or something soft wrapped around my left arm.

I brought it up against my chest and held it there. Blood, water and glass were everywhere.

"You missed the artery, thank god, but you're going to need stitches," Coach said. "And there's some glass in the wound."

I nodded.

"Come on." He helped me stand. "Let's get you out of here."

Coach gave me a warm-up suit to pull on over my bathing suit and drove me to the hospital. He said the school had phoned my parents. But he would stay with me until they could get there.

We had a couple of chairs against the wall in the waiting room. There were a lot of moms there with little kids, one older woman with her arm in a sling. One man kept bending forward and groaning like his stomach hurt. Nurses storm-walked back and forth along the hallway, carrying clipboards and talking fast. And every few minutes, the loudspeaker went off.

"Paging Doctor Patil to the OR, paging Doctor Patil. Housekeeping, line one. Housekeeping, line one."

The towel was still wrapped around my arm. The bleeding seemed to have slowed down. "Feeling better?" Coach asked. "Want to tell me what happened?"

"The door got stuck," I found myself saying.

"Stuck." He frowned. "You and I both know that door doesn't stick. Try again."

I looked at my feet. At the grungy floor.

"Sometimes they go too far," he muttered. "What if I hadn't been there?"

I got called in sooner than I expected. The bleeding had pretty much stopped. The doctor sent me for an X-ray of my hand.

I had to sit in a wheelchair for the trip to radiology. Hospital policy, the nurse said. Coach pasted on a lame attempt at a smile and called me "Hot Wheels."

"You don't have to stay," I said. "My parents will be here soon."

"Nonsense." He patted me on the shoulder. "I'm here for you, Bram. You never doubt that, okay?" He insisted on walking down to radiology with me, even though the intern wouldn't let him push the chair.

Partway down a long pale-green hallway, his footsteps stopped. "Damn it," he muttered.

I turned to see what was wrong, but he wasn't looking at me. He was looking at a well-dressed Asian couple, maybe my parents' age, walking down the hall. The woman's arm was linked through the man's. They saw Coach and froze.

"Coach Gordon," the man said.

"Mr. Tam," Coach said. He bent his head to them. His hands were clasped together in front of him, like at a funeral, and he shifted his weight from one foot to the other.

The woman's eyes skated over me. She was very thin.

The man rubbed her back. "We've just been visiting the Blackburns," he said. His voice was even, but his eyes bored into Coach. The Blackburns were Abby and Jeremy's parents. I leaned forward.

"I didn't realize you knew each other," Coach said.

"Jeremy is a good boy," the woman said. "He's kept in touch—" She didn't so much finish her sentence as lose her voice midway.

Her husband wrapped his arm around her. He nodded to Coach without speaking, and the two of them drifted away. We made it the rest of the way to the radiology waiting room.

Coach sat down beside me. He kept clearing his throat and rubbing his right knee. "Didn't realize they knew each other," he mumbled.

"Coach, were those Marcus Tam's parents?" I asked.

He blinked and looked at me as if he had forgotten I was there. "How do you know about Marcus?"

"It was in the news," I pointed out. Something kept me from admitting Jeremy had told me the story.

"Yeah." He cleared his throat again. "Yeah, of course it was. I tell you, Bram, that was a real tragedy. That boy had potential."

And parents. Somehow I had never thought about him having parents. "It was alcohol poisoning, right?" I asked.

He nodded and wiped his palm over his face. "There's not a day goes by I don't wonder what might have happened if I'd been at that party."

The lie felt like a splash of cold water. I grabbed the arms of my wheelchair. He had lied, right to my face. So what else was a lie?

I wanted to talk to Abby. We needed to decide what to do with the photo.

Coach was still talking. "You know how kids are though. They do their own thing, don't want an old coot like me hanging around. Still, I wish one of them had told me what they were planning."

His voice trailed off, but he glanced at me out of the corner of his eye.

"I don't think kids usually invite teachers to parties," I said.

"No," he said, rubbing his knee again. "No, I guess you're right."

Mom appeared soon after that. Her forehead was creased. Storrs was over an hour away, and she hated highway driving. I stood and hugged her. She felt smaller than when I'd last seen her, but she smelled the same. It made me want to hold her tighter.

She thanked Coach for taking care of me.

"Not at all, Mrs. Walters, not at all," he said. "We're like family at Strathmore." He patted me on the shoulder.

I wondered what the Tams thought about the Strathmore family. It hadn't helped Marcus much.

chapter twenty-one

It was midafternoon by the time I went out for a late lunch with Mom and reassured her that I was fine and, no, I didn't know why the sauna door stuck. And, yes, I'd never go into the sauna again. After she finished giving Coach and the headmaster a piece of her mind, there was only an hour left of class. The sauna was off-limits to everyone, pending a safety inspection and new glass.

Mom kissed me goodbye. I had gym, and the headmaster had suggested I take a study period instead. So I grabbed a few books and headed to the library. I set myself up in a back corner and opened my science textbook, but I couldn't concentrate.

There was no way the sauna was an accident. I gave up studying and headed to the newspaper archives. I found all the articles I could from three years ago, when Marcus had died.

It made for interesting reading. Not so much the headlines themselves, although the press had Marcus as a tragic victim one day and a reckless partier the next. It was more how suddenly the headlines disappeared. There was talk of a lawsuit against the school and a police investigation. Some big-shot lawyer was called in as a consultant to the school, and then...nothing.

Nothing at all.

I put the papers away and returned to my science textbook. The diagram swam in front of my eyes, colored lines and labels swirling and making no sense.

None of this made any sense.

Coach had helped me when I was hurt.

Coach had been at the party. He had lied about it.

Jeremy was going to tell the truth about Coach being at the party. Someone had tried to kill Jeremy.

Someone with a green car. Nate's father had a green car. Nate had access to it. But Nate hadn't even been on the team the year Marcus died.

If Coach had nothing to do with what happened to Jeremy, was it right to ruin his career over something that happened years ago? Better to find out who was really behind the attack on Jeremy. One of the Sharks? Nate? Steven? Or just some stranger? Maybe the police would find the guy. Maybe this whole thing would go away.

But...three years ago or not, Marcus's parents had lost their son. That story had gone away too. I had seen that for myself, in the library's newspapers. Didn't his family deserve some answers?

And who had locked me in the sauna? I slammed my book shut. It was nearly five o'clock—I'd been in the library for more than two hours. Droid would go into shock if he knew.

I had time to drop off my books before dinner. I headed up to my room, nodding to a group of freshmen I passed in the hall. A couple of them eyed the gauze on my arm like they were waiting for the stitches to unravel and blood to gush through. Word must have spread.

The door was partially open, and the room was dark. The glow of Droid's computer was visible from the hall. I shouldered on the light switch. "You'll wreck your eyes," I said.

"Thanks, Mom." Droid tapped a few keys before spinning around to face me. "So...suicide via sauna door? Very dramatic. And original."

"Ha ha." I dropped my books on my bed.

"Dude. I'm glad you're okay." He looked at me seriously for a moment. "Do you think this is because of...you know?"

The bedroom door was still open. I glanced at it and nodded, putting a finger to my lips. Droid spun over and kicked the door closed like a desk-chair ninja.

"Yeah, I do," I said, sitting down on the corner of my bed. "There were a few Sharks in the pool this morning. Not Steven, but those guys will do whatever he says."

"Was it, you know, a warning? Or are we playing for keeps now?" His voice was light, but the frown lines across his forehead were new.

I shook my head. "I didn't wait to see if they'd come back and let me out."

"Clearly. Because obviously, you're Superman." There was an edge to his voice now. "Do you think maybe it's time you and Girl Sherlock told the police about the photo? I only ask because if you get yourself killed, I'll need to look for a new roommate."

"Nobody's going to—" I was going to say kill me. But after the sauna, after what had happened to Jeremy, how could I be sure? Maybe it wasn't Coach, but somebody wanted to keep what happened to Marcus a secret. And maybe the only way to stop the insanity was to do what they were afraid of—make the photo public, no matter what happened to Coach as a result.

It was time to talk to Abby, before anything else happened.

I pulled my cell phone out of my pocket and paced while it rang. And rang. Finally her voice mail clicked through.

I punched off my phone. So she wasn't answering—it could mean anything. It could mean she didn't have her cell phone with her...but she always had it. Her brother was in the hospital. She never let it be out of reach.

Maybe she wasn't answering because she was pissed off at me for holding her up on the photo thing.

"Can I borrow your phone?" I asked Droid.

Wordlessly, he handed it over. I fumbled my way through Abby's number. I was used to calling from my address book, not punching the numbers in. The first time, I got it wrong. The second time, it rang to her voice mail again.

"It's probably nothing," Droid said. "She might be in the can."

I nodded and sent a text, telling her to call me. But just like in the sauna, I couldn't quiet the feeling that something wasn't right.

chapter twenty-two

Droid and I were halfway downstairs on the way to dinner when Steven and Nate caught up to us. They asked if I had a minute.

"Not really," I said. I wanted to get through dinner fast and try phoning Abby again. If I didn't hear from her tonight, I was going over to Wallingford. She had the photo, and we needed to decide what to do with it.

"It's important," Steven said, blocking my way.

"Easy," Nate said, putting a protective hand on my shoulder. "Bram knows what's up. He'll hear us out. Right, Bram?"

Droid and I exchanged glances. "You want me to stay?" he asked.

I shook my head. "It's okay. Save me a spot." If I didn't show up, he'd know something was wrong.

Droid continued downstairs. Steven, Nate and I waited on the landing until everyone had gone. The landing had a stained glass window, but it was already dark outside.

I crossed my arms over my chest. "What's up?"

"You've been asking some questions lately. Hanging around with Jeremy's sister. Anything you want to tell us?" Steven asked.

"That it's none of your business who I hang out with," I said, moving closer to the stairs.

Nate leaned against the window ledge. "Down boy," he said. "We're here to help you. You said something about having proof that Coach was at that party.

This wouldn't happen to be a photo you got from Jeremy, would it?"

I grabbed the banister. "How do you know about that?"

He smiled. "I'm resourceful. All I want to say is, it's better for everyone if that photo never existed. What's the big deal anyway? It was three years ago."

"You weren't even there," I said. "What does any of this have to do with you?"

"Coach is a friend of Nate's father," Steven said.

The friendly look vanished from Nate's face. "Shut it," he said. He turned back to me. "Coach came to my father for help. Dad was able to...guide the investigation, so that things worked out best for everyone."

I thought of the Tams, back at the hospital. "Everyone."

Nate nodded. "And now all we need to do is make sure that the photo disappears. You can help me with that, right, Bram?"

"I don't have it," I said. I was glad I had given it to Abby for safekeeping.

"We know," Steven said.

My mouth went dry. The only way they could know that I didn't have the photo anymore was if they knew I had given it to Abby. Had they seen me hand it to her? Or had they gotten to her somehow? Was this why she hadn't answered her phone?

"We're asking about copies," Nate said. "You didn't copy it, did you? Or scan it, or do anything silly like that?"

I shook my head.

"So you won't mind if we check your room? As teammates and all."

My heart pounded. I had to find Abby. I had to make sure she was all right. My hands were sweaty. I fumbled for my keys and handed them to Nate. "Here!" I said. "Knock yourselves out."

I ran downstairs to the refectory. Droid was at our usual table, talking technology with his friends. Red Cap was sitting with them. I did a double take.

"Dude," Droid said, spotting me. "All is well?"

I shook my head. "They're searching the room," I said. "Take your friends, grab a teacher, don't go alone, but don't let them hurt your computer. You have to send that picture to the police as soon as you can. Tell them everything. I'm going to find Abby."

His face paled. "On it," he said.

As I left, Droid said something to Red Cap, who nodded. At least Droid would have some muscle on his side.

I raced for the bike rack, but someone had slashed my tires. Mumbling an apology to Droid, I took his bike instead. It was time to talk to the one man who might have some answers. Coach.

chapter twenty-three

I remembered the way to Coach's house from when Abby and I had gone there looking for a green car. When we didn't find the car, I had thought that was proof of Coach's innocence.

I had been an idiot.

It took me about twenty minutes to get there. I dialed Abby's phone twice more on the way. No answer.

It was nearly seven thirty by the time I reached Coach's house. The streetlights made the pale yellow siding look washed out and ghostly. No Halloween decorations here, even though the big day was tomorrow.

I knocked at the door.

Coach's wife answered. I had seen her before. She was at the first-day-of-school barbecue. She had short dark hair and wore a tracksuit. "Yes?" she said, out of breath.

"I need to see Coach," I said.

Her face sharpened. "You're from the school."

I nodded. "Please," I said. "It's important."

"What's going on?" Coach's voice carried from somewhere inside. His wife bit her lip and glanced over her shoulder. Her hand moved on the door, as if she wanted to close it.

"Coach!" I shouted. "It's me. Bram."

Coach appeared in the hall behind his wife. "It's all right," he said, putting his hand on her back. "I'll deal with this." She nodded, then disappeared down the hall and through a door.

He was red-faced and sweaty. When he let me into the house, I saw moving boxes stacked in the living room. There was a smell of dust and cardboard.

"Are you moving?" I asked.

"It's time for a change," Coach said shortly. "What can I do for you, Bram?"

I took a breath. "I need to know if you've seen Abby. Jeremy's sister."

He wiped his palm over his face. "No, I haven't seen her. You came all the way out here to ask me this?"

"I can't find her," I said. "She's not answering her phone."

"Why on earth—what does this have to do with me? Does the school know you're here? They can't." He shook his head. "I'll give you a ride back. We'll talk on the way."

"Coach." I stood firm, not stepping back when he moved toward the door. "I thought she might have come to talk to you. About a photo."

"Jesus, Bram, my wife," he whispered. "Do you know what that sounds like?" He looked anxiously over his shoulder. "I'm going to run Bram back to the school, honey," he called. "I'll be right back."

He ducked back into the house, saying something about a phone call. I wheeled Droid's bike toward Coach's gray Jetta. And there, on the driveway, I spotted a flash of silver. A silver cuff earring, like the one Abby wore. My breath caught.

I pocketed the earring just as Coach came out of his house. "You're sure Abby wasn't here?" I tried to sound casual.

"I already told you, didn't I? That bike won't fit in the trunk. We'll have to use a bungee cord." He popped the trunk.

I pasted a smile on my face. "Sorry to bother you, Coach," I said. "I guess it was stupid. I think I'll just ride back to the school after all. Don't want to put you out of your way."

"Stupid? That's one word for it," he said, rummaging around inside the dark trunk. "But I'm going to see you back to school safely. We'll discuss this tomorrow, with the headmaster."

My brain was spinning. Abby had been here. Coach was lying again. What had she said to him? What had he done?

"I know you were at the party," I said. "I've seen proof. I didn't want to believe you had anything to do with what happened to Jeremy. But now I'm not so sure. So could you please tell me the truth?"

He straightened and looked at me. "What's the truth, Bram? Yeah, I messed up. But what about all the kids I've helped? Isn't that the truth too?"

"Did you try to kill Jeremy?"

"I had nothing to do with what happened to Jeremy." He crossed his arms. "I didn't even realize, at first, that it was about Marcus."

"So you know who did it." I leaned forward. "Tell me. You owe it to Jeremy. You owe it to Marcus, Coach."

He shook his head. "Some kids here have a real shot, you know? You're one of them, but there have been others too. I told myself I owed it to them to keep coaching. Not to let one mistake end my career. To keep…"

He leaned on the car, frowning, but his eyes were unfocused. He seemed to have run out of words. He wasn't a champion. He was a sad old man.

"Coach," I said. "Where's Abby? Is she in trouble? I know she was here." I put my hand in my pocket and felt the earring.

He rubbed his palm over his face again. "Abby? I dropped her off back at her school. She wanted me to go to the police, to come clean. I told her I'd think about it. I needed to...there were things I needed to do. People I needed to talk to, first."

"She's not at the school, is she?" My mouth filled with a bitter taste. I threw one leg over Droid's bike, ready to go. "I'm calling the police."

"Bram, I–" He stopped. A dark car eased onto his street. "I'm sorry."

The car rolled closer. A chill worked its way down the center of my bones. I looked at Coach, then back at the car. Coach reached for me, but I took off.

I pedaled down the street in the dark. The car followed.

chapter twenty-four

My heart was pounding hard. My palms were damp. Was this how it was for Jeremy? Knowing what was coming, trying to get away?

I pedaled faster. The car matched my speed. The engine revved once, startling me into a swerve. Sweat pooled under my helmet and trickled down my face. I wiped it away from my eyes.

They wouldn't dare try anything here. There were too many houses around. All I had to do was stay where the houses were—but I couldn't make it all the way back to Strathmore that way.

I started across a street, then turned right. Tires squealed. The car was still with me.

There wasn't much traffic at this time of night. I headed for busier roads. Ahead, there was a gap between subdivisions where train tracks crossed the street I was on. I heard the distant rumble of a train coming.

I crossed the tracks. The car crossed behind me. I kept going, swung around the block and headed back to the tracks again.

After the barriers were lowered across the road, there would be a moment before the train appeared. I could slide under the barrier and leave the car stranded on the other side of a train.

At the train crossing, the red lights flashed. The signal clanged and the wooden barriers lowered themselves into place. The train was coming now. I saw it. A black metal beast, bearing down fast. I raced toward the tracks. I could get there first.

I could dodge the wooden barrier and squeeze by the train. I—

I couldn't.

I braked hard, falling, sliding under the barrier, scraping to a stop inches away from the rails as the train whizzed by. My front tire crossed the rail. I rolled away from the bike. Sparks flew as the train devoured the front wheel. I closed my eyes, turned my face away from the deafening noise. A harsh metallic breeze flew past me, and my heart thumped in my ears.

Pain shot up from my right ankle. I pushed onto my hands and knees.

The car rolled up to the crossing, headlights pinning me down. I panted, trying to crawl. There was nowhere to go. The train kept rumbling by.

Car doors opened. Two shadowy shapes stepped out. One was tall, and both were broad-shouldered. Built like swimmers.

My ankle throbbed. I straightened, still on my knees but facing them.

"Pond scum," Nate said. He had been driving. "For a minute there, I thought you were going to do us a favor."

chapter twenty-five

"One good shove," Nate said. The train flashed by. I narrowed my eyes, ready to move.

"Don't," Steven said. "Your dad said. It'll be clean and professional. No way to trace it back to us, right? We get rid of Bram, get rid of the photo and Jeremy's computer. And we go on, like...like nothing ever happened."

"Shut up," Nate said. But he stepped away from me. "It doesn't matter. The others will be here soon."

I snuck my hand into my coat pocket and felt for my cell phone, hoping the train would cover the sound of dialing 9-1-1.

"What's he doing?" Nate asked. Steven yanked on my arm. My hand flew out of my pocket and my phone clattered onto the road.

Nate laughed and kicked it under the train.

The caboose raced away. We were alone. Not for long though. A dark sedan pulled up and a short wiry man got out

"This the kid?" he asked. "Get him in the trunk. Meet us down by the dock."

I fought and yelled, but there was no one around. They threw me into the trunk. I banged on the lid and kicked at the sides. As we bounced over the train tracks, I cushioned my head between my arms to keep it from slamming against the trunk's lid.

I felt for a safety latch, a way to open the trunk, but there was nothing. The trunk smelled greasy and old. The fabric beneath me was caked and stiff with something. My fingers curled away from it.

Maybe twenty minutes passed before we stopped. I braced myself, ready to come out fighting. But when the trunk finally opened, it wasn't Nate and Steven looking at me. It was the wiry, narrow-faced man. He had a handgun pointed at me. I stared at it and forgot to breathe.

Nate and Steven stood behind him. "Get up," Nate said.

I swallowed twice before speaking. "What's going on? Who's he?"

There was a click from the gun. I sat up. In the end, Steven had to help me out of the trunk. I was shaking. Gunmetal cold.

The air smelled of salt. We were in an empty parking lot. No lights, just the moon, and even that kept dodging behind clouds. Forest crowded up against one side of the parking lot, and the other side was a park. But straight ahead, the way I was facing, was water. We were at some kind of beach. At the bottom of the parking lot was a boat ramp.

It was quiet, almost peaceful, with the waves rushing to shore.

My body prickled, every nerve tensed to run.

"Take him to the boat," Nate said.

Steven nodded and helped me hobble along the uneven pavement, past the boat ramp. The parking lot narrowed to a sidewalk through the park. Nate went first, then Steven and I together, me hopping awkwardly. The guy with the gun followed. I shivered in the damp, cool air.

Ahead and to the right, a narrow, wooden dock stuck out into the water. A motorboat loomed at the end. I tried to breathe deep, tried to calm down. I could see West Haven across the bay. We had to be near Lighthouse Park. The bay opened into Long Island Sound. Where were they taking me?

"Do you like boats, pond scum?" Nate asked.

I stumbled and bit the inside of my mouth. Blood. I spat.

Nate glared.

"If I meant it like that," I said. "I'd have hit your shoes." My voice came out higher than

I wanted. I couldn't catch my breath, and I couldn't make my pulse settle down. Every time I pictured the gun, my hands shook.

The moon slid behind another cloud, and I tripped. Steven stopped me from falling, but he didn't say anything. He smelled of sweat and startled at every sound.

"Who is that guy?" I whispered.

Steven turned his face away.

We stepped onto the dock as the moon came out again. Some of the boards creaked. I stared at the spaces between the slats and into the inky water below.

It took thirty-one steps to reach the boat. The ocean smell of salt was strong, and the wind had picked up, pushing waves to shore. Sea spray froze to my skin. The boat reared up and down, rubber bumpers protecting it from the dock.

It was a ski boat, but larger than any I had ever seen. The pointed front was covered by a canvas tarp, fastened into place with snaps. A chrome rail ran around the edge, maybe four inches off the side of the boat. There was a windscreen to protect the front seats. The back half of the boat was open to the sky. Four leather seats sat in the middle of the boat with their backs together facing front and back, and two more were at the very back beside the large motor. Nearly everything inside and outside of the boat was black.

"Not just anyone gets a ride," Nate said. "Must be your lucky day."

The man with the gun looked relaxed, almost bored. He caught me staring at him. "Nothing personal, kid," he said. But he kept the gun trained on me.

I tried to step up into the boat, and my ankle collapsed. Steven barely kept both of us out of the water.

Water.

I couldn't outrun them, but I was a damned good swimmer. It was a dark night. If I waited for the right moment, I might have a chance.

I straightened my shoulders and drew my first full breath since I'd seen the gun.

chapter twenty-six

"If you want him in the boat, you'll have to help," Steven said to Nate. He hadn't said anything since the train tracks. His voice creaked.

"You're not in charge here," Nate said. Steven flinched, but Nate hopped into the boat.

He grabbed my arm and yanked. I fell into the boat face-first, landing half on the floor and half on the rear-facing seats.

The wrench to my ankle sent a bolt of pain up my leg.

I rolled over to face Nate. "You're a big man, aren't you? As long as you've got Daddy's hired gun to back you up." I watched the man with the gun. The line of his mouth turned up a little when I insulted Nate.

"Shut up," Nate said. "Do you even know what's going to happen to you?" The boat rocked up and down over the waves, bumping against the dock with a little thud each time.

My heart raced. I kept my eyes on the gunman. "You're going to take me for a nice boat ride, and we'll have a picnic."

Nate turned red. "You're going to New York. Don't you get it? My father's connected. He's freaking loaded. Do you even know what that means? You're going to New York, and no one's ever going to find your body."

The words hit me in the chest. My hands closed on nothing, and I felt like I was falling all over again.

But Nate smiled. A victory smile. And in that second, I hated him more than I'd ever thought possible. My hate was hot and alive, deep inside me. I clung to it.

"What do you care?" I asked. "Coach is leaving. That's what this was about, wasn't it? Hanging on to the swim coach that's in your daddy's pocket?"

"Enough," the gunman said. "Get him inside."

Nate pointed to the front of the boat. There was a crawl space under the canvas tarp. "In there," he said.

I looked up at the gunman, making it clear that I thought he was in charge, not Nate. He nodded. I wasn't going to crawl in there like a dog. I stood, using the chairs for support, and Nate had to step out of my way so I could reach the front of the boat.

I dropped into the driver's seat, glared at Nate and then shoved myself into the crawl space backward, so I could see out.

I had about two and a half feet of height between the floor of the boat and the canvas tarp ceiling. Not enough to sit up.

I lay on my side, partly curled, and propped myself up, watching the others. The boat floor smelled musty. I had room to move around, but not to straighten.

Nate climbed out of the boat, telling Steven to watch me.

Steven sat in the front passenger's seat and stared at me. His Adam's apple moved up and down as he swallowed again and again. His knuckles were white where he gripped the leather seat.

"Help me," I mouthed.

He shook his head, a small, tight movement. I was on my own.

Nate and the other man stood at the end of the dock. Nate kept glancing back at the shore and then at his watch.

I felt around. Two benches ran along either side of me and came to a point at the front of the boat. There was a bit of room between the tops of the benches and the tarp—maybe six inches or more. Enough room to open the benches if I got the chance later. Maybe there was something in there I could use. Life jackets.

Energy coiled through my body. I was ready to fight. All I needed was a chance.

"They're here." Nate's voice cut over the wind and waves. I craned my neck to see better. Footsteps thudded on the dock.

"She's coming around," a deep voice said.

"Too bad for her," Nate answered.

A large man stepped into view. Abby was flung over his shoulder, unconscious. My throat clenched.

At a sign from the man with the gun, Steven stood. The large man passed Abby down to him. Steven's face was blank—too blank. He looked shell-shocked. Even while he was easing Abby into his seat, he didn't look at her. She moaned and blinked, tried to sit up, then slowly slumped down again.

"Not there," the large man said. He had red hair and, like the smaller man with the gun, wore black. "In front with the other kid. I told you, she's coming around. I don't want any trouble in the boat."

"If there's trouble in the boat, you shoot them," Nate said.

The red-haired man chuckled. "Your daddy's getting sick of cleaning up after you," he told Nate. "Try and be a good boy."

"Enough," said the wiry man. "Get her inside."

Nate leered at me. "It's your lucky day, pond scum. Cop a feel for me."

Steven slid Abby into the opening. Her bent legs hung out from under the tarp.

"I'm going to kill him," I whispered to Steven. "I'm going to kill both of you."

He turned his blank stare on me, then disappeared back up with the others.

It was dark under the tarp. I heard the waves, felt the boat rock, heard Abby's breathing. There were thuds, maybe people getting into or out of the boat, and then someone's legs appeared in the driver's seat. "Keep them covered." It was the red-haired man's voice, the deeper one. "I don't want any problems."

"You drive, I'll take care of it," said the other man. He took the back-facing seat on the passenger side of the boat but faced forward. His right hand rested on his knee. Moonlight gleamed off the barrel of his handgun.

Nate and Steven weren't in the boat.

The motor started, vibrating through the hull and through my skin. The sound drowned everything out.

I lay crunched into the very front of the boat, sideways. Abby's head and shoulders rested against my hip. The boat started to move. Abby stirred, and I shook her shoulder. "Abby. Can you hear me? You need to wake up." I was counting on the motor to cover the sound of my voice.

"Bram?" She tried to sit up, but the canvas tarp was in the way. "Where–?"

"Stay still. Don't freak out, okay? We're in a boat."

"Nate," she said. "He–"

"Is an absolute psychopath and deserves to die," I said. "But right now we're in trouble. Listen, okay?"

She nodded. I told her what had happened as quickly as I could. She shuddered when I mentioned the gun.

"We have to swim for it," I said. "We'll wait until the moon goes behind a cloud. But soon, while we're close to shore. We dive under and stay under as long as we can. It's dark. Once they lose us, they won't find us."

She nodded again and pulled her legs in tight. "So they get used to not seeing me," she said. It was a good thing she was small. It was cramped, far worse than the car trunk had been. But now, on top of the musty boat air, I smelled Abby's perfume. Oranges. It made me feel better. My body was warm where she pressed against it. There were two of us. We had a chance.

"We need a distraction," I said. "So we can pop the snaps and get out without getting shot." Swimming the sound in the dark, in cold water and with an injured ankle, was crazy. We needed everything else to go perfectly.

"Here." She wiggled around, reaching for something, and then pressed something small and flat into my hand. Her two-inch

Swiss Army knife. "It's funny. Jeremy was the one who gave this to me. We won't need to pop the snaps. We can slit the tarp. It'll be quieter."

I popped up one snap so I could peer outside and watch for a cloud to cross the moon. Abby leaned back and cracked open the benches to rummage inside for anything we could use. We had to move slowly so they wouldn't notice. With each minute, my heart pounded faster.

"Life jackets?" she asked.

They would help us swim, but they would also make us an obvious target. Reluctantly, I said no. I would get us to shore. I had to.

Abby gasped. "Bram!"

"What?"

"I found our distraction."

chapter twenty-seven

We had taken off our shoes and jackets. That was as much as we could manage without drawing attention.

I peered through the open snap. The tiny crack of moonlight disappeared. "Now," I said.

Abby slid her knife through the tarp, making a large, L-shaped flap that would open to the driver's side to make it harder for the skinny guy to get a clear shot. I held the edges together.

Abby had wedged one of the benches open with a life jacket. She reached in to snip the wire that led to the boat's head-lamp. That was our distraction. It would also make it harder for them to find us once we were in the water.

"It won't cut," she whispered.

I shoved my arm into the opening and fumbled for the wire. Abby put my hand on it. I grabbed it and yanked.

Someone shouted, but Abby and I were already moving. I grabbed the chrome hand-rail with one hand. Abby held the other. We hurled ourselves into the water.

The cold shocked my muscles still. I wanted to kick and claw my way to the surface, but I swam down to avoid the propeller blades. Down and away from where we had splashed in. If they shot at us, I never knew it. I just swam down and down with Abby, until my lungs ached and Abby's hand tugged at mine.

We surfaced. I sucked in air. Abby was coughing. I gripped her with one arm, using the other arm and my good leg to tread water. I had to kick with the bad ankle to keep us on the surface in two-foot waves. It hurt, but we were alive.

"You okay?" I asked. She coughed. "Abby! You okay?"

"Cold," she finally managed.

"I know." My teeth and bones ached with it. I could hear the roar of the motor. The taillight darted back and forth. They were looking for us. "We have to go under again, okay?"

We dove. The cold numbed my skin. I concentrated on kicking, on gliding. On Abby's hand in mine. We surfaced again. All I smelled, all I tasted, was salt.

"I c-c-can't. C-c-c-can't d-do th-that anymore," Abby said, when we surfaced the fourth time. Her teeth chattered.

"It's okay," I said. "They're far enough away." When the next swell carried us up, I glanced around until I saw city lights. Far away. My heart sank.

"Is th-that home?" Abby asked.

Connecticut or New York, I didn't care. It was land. "Yeah," I said. "Don't let go."

We swam, always touching each other. Sometimes a lopsided breaststroke, sometimes on our backs. Moving warmed me a little, but not enough. The moon slipped in and out of clouds.

We were swimming on our backs the first time she went under. No splashing, no coughing, just a quiet, sudden sinking and her hand limp in mine. "Abby!" I hauled her up.

She blinked and coughed. "Bram?" Her voice was thick and slurred. "Where are we?"

I wanted to cry. My eyes stung. "Don't do this," I whispered. I couldn't swim for both of us. I was so tired. My arms and legs ached. My clothes were heavy, and my ankle was a dull throb. The shoreline was still so far away.

Abby sank again.

"Tired," she said, after I pulled her up and she stopped coughing.

I looked at the lights. Too far away. I swallowed. "It's okay," I told Abby. "Just kick your feet." I hauled her into a lifeguard tow, my arm across her chest, her head on my shoulder. And I swam.

The cold and the waves, the repeated motion of swimming, it all numbed me. The moon slid into and out of sight. I measured time that way. Moon seconds, long and slow. I forgot where I was and what I was doing. My body kept moving without me.

I drifted into the dark. And then cold water closed over my face, splashed into my mouth and nose, choked me. I woke up, tightened my hold on Abby, found the city lights and kept swimming.

I drifted again and didn't come back until I felt hands tugging at me, shaking me. I coughed water from my burning throat and looked into Abby's face, pale as the moon.

"Don't drown," she said. "Don't drown."

"I won't," I promised. We swam together for a while until I felt her sinking, and then I carried her again.

I don't know how long I was in shallow water before I realized it. Sand and rock ground against my skin. A beach. I crawled a few feet, pulling Abby.

A bright light shone in my eyes. Yellow. It wasn't the moon. I blinked and focused three times before I understood that it was a streetlamp. There was a boardwalk running along the beach. Too far away.

I lay down in the wet sand, pulled Abby close and slept.

chapter twenty-eight

I woke up in a hospital room, warm and dry, with an IV needle stuck in my arm. Mom and Dad were there. And, after the nurses cleared it, the police arrived. An early-morning jogger had found us and called 9-1-1.

I told them the whole story, over and over, until my throat hurt. I found out later that I wasn't allowed to see Abby. They had to make sure our stories matched.

I also learned Steven had called the Coast Guard and had them out looking for us. I wasn't sure how to feel about that.

Coach made it most of the way to Mexico before they caught him. He and his wife had a lot of cash stashed in their car. More money than you make coaching varsity sports. It was all part of Nate's father's cleanup, I guess. Maybe when you have a lot of money, you can go through life not caring who you hurt. Or maybe it's not about the money. Maybe it's just who you are, your character.

The Coast Guard found the guys in the boat. Last I heard, the police were still looking for Nate and his father.

I didn't find this all out at once. It happened bit by bit, over days and weeks. But something else happened before I left.

Mom came in. She was smiling, but her eyes were damp. "Jeremy wants to see you," she said. "If you're ready."

They took me in a wheelchair up to the seventh floor. I could have walked with crutches (my ankle was sprained, not broken), but the nurses said it was hospital policy. I wasn't very good with the crutches anyhow.

Jeremy's room had peach-colored curtains, just like mine. Abby was already there, along with her dad. Her dad ducked out of the room when I appeared. He squeezed my shoulder as he passed.

Abby had ditched her wheelchair and was standing beside Jeremy's bed. "He's doing a lot better," she said, almost defensively. When I got close, I saw why.

He looked terrible. His face was swollen and discolored. He wore a cast on one arm and both legs, and he breathed shallowly, like it hurt. But he was awake.

"Just a few minutes," the nurse said.

I nodded. I stared at Jeremy. My tongue dried up.

"Thank you," Jeremy said, hardly moving his jaw.

I nodded. "I wish I'd figured it out sooner," I said. "I wish—"

But Jeremy shook his head, then winced. "Did good."

Abby came around beside me and took my hand. Jeremy's eyes widened. "Again?" he asked.

Abby shrugged. "Get out of bed first. Then worry about who I'm dating."

Jeremy groaned. Abby and I decided to let him get some rest.

We had some catching up to do.

chapter twenty-nine

It's March. I'm on the starting block for state-wide junior varsity finals, men's freestyle.

Abby and Jeremy are in the stands with my parents. Jeremy isn't walking well yet, so they're in the wheelchair-accessible seating at the top of the stands. Abby waves. Jeremy's wearing his Strathmore uniform and his varsity swimming jacket.

Droid is with our new coach and the rest of the team. He's wearing his Sharks swim cap.

My lane is in front of me, blue water rippling. This is my world. I lean forward and let my fingers skim the starting block. I'm focused. Ready.

I'm on the team. I'm a Shark, but I'll never call myself that, not after everything that happened.

I'm not a shark. I'm something better, stronger, faster.

Me.

Acknowledgments

In this, as in all writing projects, huge thanks must go to my wonderful writing group, Critical Ms. When *Haze* was being edited, CM included Anne Louise Currie, Kimberly Gerson (the Americanisms expert), Kathy Himbeault, Jason Pyper, Gwynn Scheltema, Jocelyne Stone, Bill Swan, Gavy Swan and Ruth Walker, but I've learned from all CMers along the way. Thanks also to those in the Mabel's Fables workshop led by Peter Carver for helping with some tricky scenes. Especially, thank you to Karen Rankin for the rescue read.

Thank you to Susan and Henry Blakeney—Sue for invaluable feedback and encouragement and cookies, and Henry for being a one-man Wikipedia when I needed it.

Cathy Gerroir, private swim teacher and coach with the Whitby Dolphins swim team, thank you for being so generous with your time and knowledge. I love your passion for swimming. This book only scratches the surface of the world you showed me.

Thank you also to Karen Hansen-Cowper of Trafalgar Castle School, and Gary Godkin of St. Andrew's College, for being so gracious and open and for taking the time to introduce me to the workings of private-school life. I came away with an even greater respect for your schools and for the people who work there.

Thank you, Alix (Dr. Alix Carter if we're being formal, but why start now?), for letting me pick your brain for the details around Jeremy's accident. It worries me how much fun you seemed to have with that.

And Mike Thomas, thanks for helping me get the weight room scenes right, and for being a great brother. But don't tell anyone I said that. Thanks also to Mike's friend Bram Peters for allowing me to borrow your name. It's a cool name. I hope you approve of the character I gave it to.

Thank you to my agent, Monica Pacheco of Anne McDermid & Associates Literary Agency, and especially to wonderful editor (and fearless rescuer of wasps), Christi Howes, and to all the team at Orca.

And finally, thank you to my family, Aaron and Sarah. For everything.

Erin Thomas is the author of several books for children and teens. She loves to read, especially stories with lots of adventure. She enjoyed learning more about swimming for *Haze*, although her own swimming career never went past a lopsided crawl. Part of the inspiration for *Haze* came from Erin's own experiences with hazing at university.

She lives in her hometown of Whitby, Ontario, with her husband, their daughter, a small gray cat and a large black dog. Both the cat and the dog hate to swim.

To learn more about Erin and her books, please visit www.erinthomas.ca.

9781554692941 pb

orca sports
Boarder Patrol
Erin Thomas

orca sports

For more information on all the books
in the Orca Sports series, please visit
www.orcabook.com.